FORBIDDEN LOVE

"You know," Tim said, "I'm starting to feel like we're some kind of Romeo and Juliet."

"We've got to do something," Patti said fiercely.

"What?"

"We've got to think of a way to talk this thing out with our parents. We can't go on like this forever, sneaking around like we're criminals or something."

"You're right," agreed Tim grimly. "We've got to take action. Only it could backfire on us, you know."

Patti sighed. "I guess that's a chance we'll just have to take."

Forbidden Love

Marian Woodruff

BANTAM BOOKS
TORONTO · NEW YORK · LONDON · SYDNEY

RL 6, IL age 11 and up

FORBIDDEN LOVE
A Bantam Book / April 1983
Reprinted 1983
Reprinted 1985

Cover photo by Pat Hill

ISBN 0-553-17843-1

Published simultaneously in the United States and Canada

Bantam Books are published by Bantam Books, Inc. Its trademark, consisting of the words "Bantam Books" and the portrayal of a rooster, is registered in U.S. Patent and Trademark Office and in other countries. Marca Registrada. Bantam Books, Inc., 666 Fifth Avenue, New York, New York 10103.

Printed in Great Britain by Hunt Barnard Printing Ltd.

O 0 9 8 7 6 5 4 3 2 1

Forbidden Love

Chapter One

"I still can't believe your dad let you take the car today," said Denise as she gazed out the window at McKinley High's red brick facade, which was coming into view.

Patti smiled at her best friend's remark. Denise knew just *how* hard Patti had had to fight to get her father's trust since she had gotten her license. It was Patti's first solo flight, and she was both thrilled and nervous.

As she stopped at the crosswalk to let a jostling stream of students cross the road, Patti sighed. "Perils of the profession, I guess. Insurance agents see so many accidents they can't help but be nervous about their own kids driving."

Denise laughed, her almond-shaped brown eyes crinkling up at the corners. "My father is so glad to be rid of one of us, if only for a few hours, that he practically throws the car keys to my sister or me."

"Lucky you."

Because she was an only child, Patti envied Denise's home life—which included two brothers and three sisters, a dog, three cats, and a talking minah bird named Rico that sounded like a hoarse Howard Cosell. Everything was thrown together in a rambling, two-story Victorian house that Patti described as pleasant pandemonium. Denise's father owned a shoe store in downtown Clinton, which was a lucky thing, he always said, since he was trying to keep a family of centipedes in shoes. Denise had inherited her sense of humor and fiery red hair from him. She had acquired her warmth from her mother, who reminded Patti of her own mom. This thought always caused Patti some sorrow. Her mother had died three years before when Patti was thirteen. She still missed her a lot, although the pain wasn't so bad as it had been at first.

Every time Patti caught herself wanting to trade places with Denise, her friend would tell her how lucky she was to live in a quiet house and have her own room where she could do whatever she wanted, such as play her records without someone screaming to stop making a racket, or where she didn't have to worry about younger brothers and sisters needing their shoelaces tied or borrowing her best lamb's wool sweater and returning it with boysenberry jam smudged all over it.

No one ever screamed at Patti. Her father wasn't the screaming type, though he would use a deep booming tone that left no doubt that he meant business. He was strict, *too* strict, Patti thought, often treating her as if she were six instead of sixteen. Even though Patti knew this was because her father cared about her and was concerned for her safety, it grated on her. She had read in a magazine once that overprotectiveness was synonymous with single parenthood.

As for brothers and sisters, Patti would gladly have traded a sweater or two for the boisterous camaraderie that abounded in Denise's house, even if the fireworks really got going there sometimes.

"What did you do to convince him, anyway?" Denise asked as she peeled the foil wrapper from a stick of sugarless gum. "Wave a magic wand or something?"

"Well—it might have something to do with the suits he wants me to pick up at the cleaners after school. Or"—her green eyes slanted in a mischievous sidelong glance—"it just might be that chocolate cake I made him in home ec the other day. Chocolate happens to be Dad's favorite."

Denise groaned, looking down at her plump but not unpleasant curves. "Please don't mention that word in my presence! I'm supposed to be on a diet, remember?"

Denise was always on a diet—usually some crazy fad diet like starving herself on grapefruit and hard-boiled eggs for a whole week—but whatever she lost she usually gained right back. A confirmed "yoyo," in Denise's own words. Patti refrained from saying anything. She thought her friend looked fine, but it was no use telling her. Anyway, Patti knew it wasn't what other people thought about you that counted, it was what you thought of yourself.

Patti knew this because of her own uncertain feelings. She got good grades, she knew she had some talent as a singer, and her friends told her she was attractive. Alone in her room she would study herself; her reflection in the mirror showing a slender girl with shiny, shoulder-length chestnut hair and wideset, greenish-gold eyes that needed only the tiniest bit of mascara to make them stand out. She didn't even mind, *really*, that her nose was a little on the stubby side or that

4

one front tooth turned in slightly. Yet even when she added up all her assets, Patti still felt insecure and awkward about herself. It wasn't that she wanted to be someone else, someone prettier or more popular or more talented—she just wished she could be more comfortable in her own skin.

And then there was the problem of her father. . . .

"I had to promise up, down, and sideways that I'd be extra careful and wouldn't go over the speed limit," she said. "Even then he gave me a twenty-minute lecture about not following other cars too closely and not parking in too-tight spots and not—"

"In other words," Denise cut in, "no fun, right?"

"Oh, well," Patti said, then sighed. "He is right, you know. It's dumb to take chances, and I do act without thinking sometimes. But still, I'm no speed demon. Dad knows that, or he wouldn't have given in, chocolate cake or no chocolate cake."

At the mention of chocolate cake again, Denise hurriedly changed the subject. "Hey, did you see the notice on the bulletin board about the spring concert? Are you still thinking of transferring out of chorus into the a cappella choir?"

Patti shrugged, her face growing warm. "I don't know. Mrs. Jaffe wants me to, but I'm not sure I'm ready."

The a cappella choir was more of an elite club than a music class, although it was graded as one. Normally Patti would have had to wait until her junior year to be eligible, but Mrs. Jaffe felt she was ready and was willing to recommend the transfer. Patti wasn't so sure. The kids in the a cappella choir were really good; in addition to the performances they gave at school, they had participated in several local concerts and had even won awards at regional choral festivals. Patti had heard that one of the local TV stations was going to televise their spring concert. Patti loved to sing—she had been doing it all her life—but the mere thought of being on television was enough to start her stomach somersaulting.

Denise reacted with indignation. "Are you kidding? You sing better than any of them. Why don't you admit the truth—you're just chicken to try out, aren't you?"

"Oh, Denise," she said, moaning, "I *want* to be in the choir, but I just don't know if I can get up and sing in front of a bunch of people. What if I have to solo?"

"Why don't you worry about that if it happens? Honestly, Patti, you have to take *some* chances if you want to get anywhere. The trouble with you is that you don't believe in yourself enough. Look at you. You're pretty, smart, talented, and, ugh, slim. And besides," she added, giving her a sly glance, "maybe it would give you a chance to get to know Tim."

Why did Denise have to bring him into it? she wondered. As if she didn't have enough to worry about already! The thought of Tim McBride, star tenor soloist of the a cappella choir, brought flames to her cheeks. Besides having a fantastic voice, he was one of the most popular—and the most gorgeous, in her opinion—boys at McKinley.

Only Denise knew about Patti's secret crush on Tim. Sometimes she was embarrassed even to have her best friend know. In addition to being a soloist in the choir, Tim, a natural actor, was the star performer in all the school plays. Having a crush on Tim McBride was a little like having a crush on a movie star. Strictly teenybopper stuff, Patti thought. Half the girls at McKinley had crushes on Tim McBride, and most of them had about as much chance of getting a date with him as they did with Harrison Ford.

On the other hand, as Denise was always ready to point out, Tim was "available," which only meant that although he had no shortage of dates, he wasn't going with anyone in particular—he had broken up with Honey Jenkins the year before. But with all of Tim's activities it didn't seem as if he had time for a steady girlfriend. Along with his many rehearsals after school, Tim was also taking voice lessons from a private tutor. In fact, the school paper had recently quoted Tim as saying that "pursuing a career in voice" was more important to him than his social life. Patti didn't know if she should be encouraged or discouraged by this fact.

She certainly didn't consider herself an expert when it came to boys. How could she be when this was only the first year her father had allowed her to date? So far she'd had exactly four dates—one with Todd Peck, who had seemed shy sitting in the back of world geography but had turned into a teenaged Mr. Hyde when he had her alone in his car. The other three dates were all with Joey Gleason, who was really very nice but very shy. The only thing they had been able to manage comfortably together were double features at the Rialto, and after three dates Patti had tired of that. The smell of popcorn still reminded her of Joey. She kept telling herself it was better to be dateless than to go out with someone she didn't like.

"*If* I decide to try out," she announced firmly, more for her own sake than Denise's, "it won't be because of Tim McBride."

Denise's round face dimpled in a smile as they headed through the gates of the parking lot. "Whatever you say, but I wouldn't be too surprised if . . ." Her voice trailed off as something in the distance caught her attention.

"Hey, Patti," she said, "could you let me off here? I see somebody I have to talk to about a history assignment."

"That somebody wouldn't be Jamie Earle, would it?" Patti said teasingly. She would have known something was up even if Denise hadn't told her. History, which had always been Denise's worst subject, was suddenly all she could talk about.

Now it was Denise's turn to blush, but her eyes sparkled merrily as she slid gracefully from the front seat of the station wagon. "Who else?" she parried. "You didn't think I meant George Washington, did you?"

Patti watched her bright red head bob off in the direction of a dark-haired boy standing near the front steps. Soon the two were talking excitedly. Patti couldn't help but feel a twinge of envy as she drove off in search of a parking space. It was obvious Denise had found someone special. *When will it be my turn?* Patti wondered, her chest tightening slightly.

She was so lost in her thoughts, she forgot to pay attention to where she was going and made a too-abrupt turn as she rounded a row of parked cars. A bright red MG was backing out in front of her, but it was too late to stop. In the horrifying split second that was left, Patti slammed her foot against the brake, her heart lurching into her throat as her front bumper connected with the sports car's rear one in a sickening crunch.

A tall, lanky boy in a navy sweatshirt catapulted from the tiny car and raced over to where she was sitting, her hands locked onto the steering wheel. She was unable to stop quivering. His face loomed in the open window, wearing an expression of tightly controlled anger that flipped to anxious concern when he saw how deathly pale she was.

"Are you all right?" he asked. She nodded, blinking back hot tears of shame as she watched his anger return. "Why didn't you honk or something? Jeez, I didn't even see you!"

Patty was trembling so hard she didn't trust herself to speak. The shock of recognizing *who* she had run into was almost worse than the moment of the crash. It was unbelievable. The kind of awful coincidence that doesn't really happen in life, only in bad movies. Of all the people at McKinley High she could have bashed into, she had to pick Tim McBride!

"I'm s-s-sorry," she stammered. "I guess I wasn't looking. It was all my fault." Her throat felt as if it were being squeezed by a giant fist. Tears spilled down her cheeks.

He softened at once and reached out to place a comforting hand on her shoulder. "Hey, I'm sorry I yelled. It could have been worse, I guess. At least no one got hurt." Then he glanced over at his car again and flinched. "It's just that I'd saved my summer money all year hoping for a car like this to come along. This is the first day I've taken it out. What rotten luck!"

Numbly Patti forced herself to climb out and inspect the damage. Her legs felt as if they might collapse at any moment. What steeled her was the thought that Tim might have to catch her if she fell. She had daydreamed about him holding her in his arms— but not like that!

She groaned as she surveyed the tangle of chrome that had once been two bumpers.

One of the MG's taillights and one of her headlights had been shattered, and part of the MG's rear end was dented as well.

"My dad is going to have a fit!" she said.

Well, that wasn't exactly true, she thought. He would be upset, but worse than that, he would be disappointed in her. That was the hard part. Just when Patti was on the verge of proving to him how grown-up and trustworthy she was, too. It was bound to set her back at least a thousand years. Now he would never think of her as more than a dumb little kid—probably even when she was old and gray haired!

Tim's thoughts echoed her own. "I know what you mean. My mom's not going to be exactly overjoyed, either. I wasn't supposed to be driving this until I got insurance. The trouble is I got this stupid ticket last year for running a stop sign, and now everywhere I've checked, the rates are so sky-high I'd have to be a millionaire to afford them. But Mom's got a friend in the business, and she was supposed to look into it this week. Wow, when she finds out about this!"

All that time Tim had been kneeling to get a closer look at the damage, but when he straightened up, Patti saw that he was only a few inches taller than she. It was the closest she had ever gotten to him, and she was surprised, for she had always imagined he would tower over her. At that distance, she was uncomfortably aware of his angular face, stunning electric-blue eyes, and dark blond curls. Her heart galloped when she realized that he was staring at her, too.

For a brief instant Patti forgot about the two cars welded together in front of them. All she could think about was the fact that she was actually standing there talking to Tim McBride. She was glad she'd worn something nice—beige culottes and a new candy-pink blouse instead of her usual jeans and T-shirt. Her pulse thudded in her ears as one corner of his mouth lifted in the cockeyed smile that was a Tim McBride trademark.

"Now I know why you look so familiar," he said. "You were in the Christmas concert." That was when Mrs. Jaffe's chorus classes had merged with the a cappella choir to perform the *Messiah*. Patti was surprised he remembered her.

"Right," she mumbled. The same voice that had soared in the *Messiah* was now sticking in her throat like a glob of peanut butter. She managed to add, "Your solos were really great."

He looked surprised. "You thought so? I

had the flu that night so I really felt I blew it. Do you ever feel like you want to take a big eraser and rub out a day of your life?"

In spite of her embarrassment, Patti found herself laughing. "How about today?"

Tim joined in, momentarily dissolving the tension that had lain between them. How could he be so nice after what she'd done? Patti wondered. She found herself thinking that having a crush on someone wasn't the same as really knowing him. Before that day, she had admired Tim from a distance—he might have been a statue she'd seen in a park and thought was beautiful. But now that she'd actually met him and seen how nice he was, Patti wished desperately for the chance to get to know him better—to see if the wild flutterings inside her could develop into something more.

She told him that her father was an insurance agent and that she would explain the whole thing to him when she got home. She was sure the company would pay for the damage to Tim's car.

Tim looked relieved. "That should smooth Mom over a little. After she gets through chewing me out, that is. You know how lawyers can be about sticking to the rules."

"Your mother's a lawyer?"

Tim grinned. "Yeah."

"That's really neat." Patti was impressed.

"It is, but try living with one sometime. You never win an argument."

"What does your father do?"

Tim shrugged. "He's a lawyer, too, but they're divorced."

Patti could have bitten off her tongue for being so nosy. She didn't even know why she'd asked—it just seemed like a natural question. She relaxed when she saw that Tim wasn't going to hold it against her.

"My mom and I live in the apartment building down the block from the courthouse," he volunteered. "It's convenient for her, and most of the time I have the place to myself, so it works out great during rehearsals. Gives us a place to study our scores and sing where there's not a bunch of kid brothers and sisters getting in the way."

Patti thought of Denise's house—how full of life and fun it was, even if it got messy and the little kids were terrors sometimes.

"I don't know," she said. "I always thought it'd be nice to have a brother or sister. Being the only one gets sort of lonely."

Tim gave her a long, thoughtful look. His blue eyes were so intense, she thought. They were like lasers cutting into her innermost thoughts. She noticed how the sun brushed the ends of his curls, turning them a fiery gold, and that one of his front teeth was crooked, just like hers.

"I guess I know what you mean," Tim admitted slowly, as if it were the first time he'd done so.

They were interrupted by the jangle of a bell in the distance, reminding them they had only five minutes to get to their first-period classes. Patti was still a little shaky about driving, so Tim offered to park the station wagon for her. Afterward she told him she would call him when she had spoken with her father.

Tim fished an old piece of paper from his wallet and scribbled something on it. "Here's my number," he said, handing it to her.

"Thanks." Patti stuffed it into her book bag, knowing she would treasure that dumb piece of paper forever, no matter how this whole thing turned out. "Well . . . see ya."

She was halfway across the parking lot when Tim yelled after her, "Hey! What's your name— I forgot to ask!"

"Patti!" she yelled back, her voice rising. "Patti Curtis!"

His eyes, even from that distance, sent goose

bumps up her back. "I'll remember that," he said, grinning.

A fragile bubble of hope rose in her. *I'll remember that.* . . . It shimmered brightly for a minute before it abruptly exploded. Of course he would remember her! After she had practically wiped him out, how could he possibly forget her?

Chapter Two

Ms. Ketchum had her back to the class as she diagramed a sentence on the blackboard. The chalk made loud clicking noises as her arm swept up and down in broad, energetic strokes. Denise leaned across her desk and hissed to get Patti's attention.

"What happened out in the parking lot?" she whispered, her eyes the size of Frisbees. "Gayle Summers told me you had some kind of accident!"

Patti rolled her eyes. "You're never going to believe it. Compared to this, *The Poseidon Adventure* was nothing." Ms. Ketchum's elbow suddenly stopped moving, and Patti added hurriedly, "I'll fill you in after class."

Ms. Ketchum turned around and fixed Patti with a long stare. She was a tall, masculine-looking woman in her mid-forties and had long black hair which she wore pulled back in a bun. A gray streak ran down the middle of her hair; it always made Patti think of a skunk. But in spite of Ms. Ketchum's appearance, and sometimes brusque manner, she was kindhearted. Patti wouldn't forget how nice Ms. Ketchum had been to her the time she had accidentally copied down the wrong homework assignment. The teacher had let her do the paper over again without marking her down a grade for being late.

"Patti." Her deep voice boomed over the classroom. "Can you tell us what the possessive and its object are in this sentence?"

Patti stared at the blackboard, trying to focus her attention on the sentence written there. Ms. Ketchum always used famous quotes for her diagraming. This time she'd picked a romantic quote by Thomas Moore.

> But there's nothing half so sweet
> as love's young dream.

She automatically thought of Tim and blushed. "Uh—is it 'love's dream'?"

"Very good, Patti." A reluctant smile tugged at the corners of her mouth. "I suppose that just goes to show that half a student's attention is better than none."

The class greeted this unexpected show of

humor with a ripple of laughter. Denise shot Patti a sympathetic look.

When the bell rang, they rushed out into the corridor together, Patti neatly sidestepping a wadded-up test paper buffeted about among the stampeding feet.

"That was really cool the way you answered that question in class," Denise said. "I would've gotten it wrong, even if I had known the answer, with those beady eyes of hers boring into me."

"Yeah, that's me—Cool Curtis." Patti gave a dry laugh. "On second thought, better make that Klutzy Curtis. I'm sure that's how Tim thinks of me."

"*Tim?*" screamed Denise. "You don't mean *the* Tim? Tim McBride? He's the one you ran into? Boy, talk about fate!"

"Bad luck, you mean," said Patti, pouring out the whole story as they made their way toward the lockers. "What gets me is how nice he was about it. I mean there I was crying on his shoulder after I'd wrecked his car—and he was consoling *me.*"

"Would you have felt better if it was all his fault?" Denise asked.

"At least I wouldn't feel so dumb."

"Look at it this way." Denise gave up fiddling with her combination lock and started banging against the locker with the heel of her hand, hoping that that might loosen it up. She was always reversing the numbers on her combination lock. "At least Tim knows who you are now. Isn't that better than not being noticed at all?"

"I'm not sure. A person could get noticed for a lot of things—for all the wrong reasons," she pointed out, "and then not be liked. Take Maryjane Watkins, for instance. She's well known by everyone who's been in PE with her—only she gained her reputation by making goals for the wrong side in soccer and hitting tennis balls over the backboard. Sometimes it's better *not* to be noticed."

"Just don't jump to any conclusions, OK?" warned Denise, wrenching her locker open at last and causing a loud bang as the door swung against its neighbor.

"Actually," Patti confessed, "I'm more worried about my father right now than Tim."

"Uh-oh, I forgot about him."

Patti shoved a pile of books inside her locker and slammed it shut. "I just wish there was some way *I* could forget."

Denise giggled. "I just thought of something—you know, about you having sort of a crush on Tim. Well, I guess this makes it official. Get it—*crush*?"

"Oh, Denise, that's awful!" Patti cried, giving her a light punch in the arm, but at least Denise had gotten her to laugh.

At noon they ate lunch in the cafeteria with Gayle and Tracy Summers, twin sisters who were as opposite from one another as night and day. Gayle was fair skinned with baby-fine blond hair; Tracy had brown eyes and black hair that hung in a thick curtain to her narrow waist. Gayle was the outgoing one, while her sister was forever struggling to overcome her shyness.

"I think I would have just rolled up into a little ball and died on the spot if it'd been me," commented Tracy as she peeled Saran Wrap from her sandwich.

"I can just see you—rolling across the parking lot with Tim in hot pursuit," Gayle said, which made them all laugh.

"How did you find out about it?" Patti asked.

"Eddie Talbot told me in chemistry. He saw you and Tim out in the parking lot right after it happened."

"Wow!" Denise exclaimed. "Eddie Talbot's got a mouth the size of the Grand Canyon. The whole school must know by now."

"Oh, that's just great." Patti could feel the milk she'd just drunk begin to curdle in her stomach. "Just what I need—a reputation as a hot-rodder. As if I won't have enough problems when my dad finds out."

"Don't worry, Patti," reassured Gayle, winking mischievously. "We'll stick up for you. If anyone calls you a hot-rodder, we'll tell them what a tortoise you really are."

"Thanks a lot," Patti mumbled, her mouth full of sandwich.

"Hey, who wants to go to the noon movie?" asked Denise. "They're showing the end of *Friday the Thirteenth, Part Two*."

Tracy made a face. "I'm not sure my stomach can handle it so soon after lunch."

"I'll go with you," Patti said. She decided a haunted summer camp might be just what she needed to take her mind off her own problems.

"Sorry, guys, I can't," put in Gayle. "I've got choir practice."

Gayle, a year ahead of Patti and Denise, sang alto in the a cappella choir, and she had been pressuring Patti to join ever since she had heard that Mrs. Jaffe wanted to transfer her. She insisted it was no different from what she was already doing in chorus, but Patti knew better. The chorus sang in front of an audience, just twice a year, and this didn't frighten her because she could think

24

of herself as only being part of one large voice. The a cappella choir, however, was much smaller, there were many solos, and the group performed frequently.

It was easy for Gayle to say that the a cappella choir was no different from chorus. With her talent and outgoing personality, she was a natural performer. Besides, all the other kids in the group were her own age.

"Mr. Reese is looking for another soprano, by the way," Gayle added nonchalantly. "The soprano section has been short ever since Laura Fineman got mono."

Patti laughed. "I get the hint. Maybe if I get mono, too, you'll stop bugging me."

Denise rolled her eyes. "I give up on you, Curtis. You're absolutely hopeless."

"You've got to think *big!*" chided Gayle.

"I agree, and I'm an expert," Denise said, grinning. "Only my problem is I've always thought *too* big." She placed her hands over her rounded stomach for emphasis. "I've got to learn to think a little smaller."

"I haven't noticed Jamie complaining," Patti observed.

Denise responded by blushing and snatching up her books and purse. "Come on, if you don't stop jabbering, we're going to be late."

*   *   *

The multi-use room, where noon movies were shown on Thursdays and Fridays, was a short distance downhill from the main school building. Patti and Denise strolled along a path lined with decades-old acacia trees, whose branches, laden with yellow blossoms, formed a thick canopy overhead. It was a warm, humid day, drowsy with the scent of newly cut grass and the droning of bees. A lot of people were sprawled on the lawn, soaking up the spring sunshine, and several skateboarders zigzagged lazily along the concrete walkways.

Inside the auditorium it was cool and dark. They found seats on the bleachers after they had paid their quarters—just in time to watch a counselor get torn apart by the dead monster. A bloodcurdling scream ripped through the room, followed by several loud groans from the audience.

Denise whispered, "This part always gets me. The first time I saw it, it took me a month to agree to go back to my summer camp. And when I finally did go back, I refused to go outside alone, after dark, all summer."

Patti giggled. "And you think I've got hang-ups."

"Speaking of hang-ups," Denise whispered, "look who just walked in."

Patti looked down and immediately spotted Tim, with a group of friends, sliding into an empty space two rows below. Her pulse quickened, and there was a funny, thick feeling in her chest. From then on Patti had difficulty in concentrating on the movie. Her eyes kept wandering to the back of Tim's head, and Denise had to elbow Patti in the ribs every time something suspenseful happened.

Nevertheless, the accident in the parking lot embarrassed Patti so that she didn't want Tim to see her. Just before the ending credits, she made an escape from the movie, mumbling some feeble excuse to Denise. But as she began groping her way down the bleachers, the lights popped on, and Patti was suddenly caught up in a surge of bodies. She lost her balance, pitching forward into a solid wall of muscle. A groan escaped her as she looked up into a familiar face.

Tim's blue eyes sparkled with amusement. "Must be in the stars for us to keep bumping into each other. Either that or somebody's put out a contract on me, and you're the hit woman."

Patti smiled self-consciously. "Do I look like a hit woman?"

"Hmmm." He gave her a long, appraising look. "Too pretty. I'd give you a mustache and thick ankles. Then—maybe."

"Would another dent in your car convince you I mean business?" Patti was astonished at herself for joking about something that wasn't the least bit funny. That was one of the crazy things about her—whenever she was nervous or something awful happened, she usually ended up cracking a joke, then hating herself for it afterward.

But Tim didn't seem to mind. "I'll pass if you don't mind," he said. "How about a Coke instead?"

"Sure. I've got a few minutes before my next class." Patti felt as if she were walking on air as she and Tim went outside and across the patio to where there was a row of vending machines.

Cokes in hand, they settled on a bench under the lacy umbrella of a Chinese elm. "Your friend Gayle tells me you're interested in joining the choir," he remarked.

So Tim has been talking to Gayle about me! Patti was so nervous she could hardly hold on to her Coke can. "Mrs. Jaffe wants me to try out, but—" She shrugged. "I don't know. Except for the chorus, I haven't done much singing in front of an audience. The time I was a singing reindeer in my sixth-grade Christmas play I almost threw up."

Tim laughed. "I'll bet you were terrific anyway."

"My parents gave me a standing ovation."

"There you go. And if you're as terrific as Gayle says you are, I'm sure Mr. Reese will consider you a welcome addition to the choir."

At the mention of Mr. Reese, Patti groaned. "I've heard he's pretty temperamental. Is it true he breaks his baton in half whenever he gets really mad?"

"Oh, don't worry about Reese. I think the reason he yells so much is that he likes the sound of his own voice. He used to be an opera singer, so it must be frustrating for him to spend all his time hanging around a bunch of amateurs like us."

"But you're not an amateur," Patti blurted out without thinking. "You're—special." As soon as she'd said it, she felt a familiar heat creep up into her cheeks. Had she revealed too much?

But Tim didn't take it that way. "Thanks. That's a nice way of putting it. Sometimes I feel like I just stand out. Do you ever feel like that? Like you don't really fit in anywhere?"

Too full of emotion to speak, Patti simply nodded, running her fingers lightly over the scarred trunk of the Chinese elm. It was a living museum of McKinley High romances, past and present. E.B. Loves J.L.—that was Elaine Baumgarten and Jimmy Lewis—they'd been going together since their freshman year and were always getting sent to the office for necking in the halls. Carved inside a lopsided heart were the names BEN AND LUCY. Patti didn't know who they were, but she wondered if they were still together and if they still attended the school. Patti imagined her own initials carved next to Tim's, then quickly brushed the thought aside, afraid Tim would read it in her face.

"We had a tree like this in our backyard before my mom and dad—before we moved," Tim mused. "It even had a tree house, and I could sit up there and see practically the whole neighborhood. I still miss that tree house sometimes—isn't that dumb?"

"No, I don't think it's dumb," Patti replied softly. "I never had a tree house, but there's this hollow down by the creek below our house where the trees grow over a kind of cave. I used to go there a lot just to be alone, or when something was bugging me and I needed time to think it out."

"Did you talk to yourself? I did."

"I sang." Suddenly Patti no longer felt shy—as if it weren't the great Tim McBride she was talking to but simply an old comfortable friend. "I made up these crazy songs because I knew no one could hear me."

"How about singing one of those crazy songs for me sometime?"

"Never!" She laughed. "But I still go to my hiding place sometimes."

The warmth in Tim's smile seemed to reach out and encircle her like an embrace. "I'd like to see it sometime—if you wouldn't mind."

Patti's throat went dry, the words sticking as she tried to speak. "I wouldn't mind," she managed in a soft, almost inaudible voice.

Tim's hand curled over Patti's, his large, warm fingers encompassing hers easily. "You know something?" he said, his electric eyes finding their way directly into her heart. "I think you and I might have more in common than a couple of banged-up bumpers, Patti Curtis."

Chapter Three

"That woman!" Frank Curtis banged his briefcase down on the coffee table. "If the company doesn't settle this case soon, I may end up in a straitjacket!"

Patti glanced up at her father from the living room floor, where she was sprawled on her stomach doing her homework. "What case is that, Dad?"

"Remember I told you about Mr. Horsnyder—the Fuller Brush salesman who's being sued by a lady who claims he backed over her prize rosebushes?"

"Is that who you're mad at—the lady with the rosebushes?" Patti went back to figuring the square root of 16,982. It was easier, she thought, than trying to come up with a comfortable way to tell her dad about the accident—especially after seeing what a great mood he was in.

"No, not Mrs. Waverly." Loosening his tie, he sank down in the easy chair by the fireplace. He was a heavyset man with strong features and crinkly salt-and-pepper hair that grew in a halo around the bald spot on the top of his head. "She's a pretty tough old bird for eighty-six, but it's her lawyer I'm talking about. A real women's libber."

"Dad," Patti said, moaning, "you're so old-fashioned!"

"What's wrong with old-fashioned, I'd like to know? At least in the old days a woman knew how to act around a man."

"What did she do that was so terrible?"

"Well, first she got mad just because I got up and offered her my chair. It *was* the best chair, after all. Then when I tried to calm her down with a compliment, she nearly bit my head off."

"What was the compliment?" Patti asked suspiciously.

There was a hint of roguishness in her father's smile. "I only said she was too pretty to be a lawyer."

"Daddy, you didn't!" Patti rolled over onto her back, pretending to be mortally wounded. "Ugh! I can't believe what a chauvinist you are!"

"None of that talk from you, young lady,"

he chided, his stern expression unable to disguise the twinkle in his eye. "We chauvinists deserve respect, too, you know."

A minute later he frowned at the books and papers scattered over the carpet. "Shouldn't you be doing that at your desk? A person can't concentrate properly lying on the floor like that."

Patti sighed. "I do some of my best concentrating on the floor," she countered, chewing the end of her pencil.

"How was school today?" he asked.

Patti cleared her throat. It was her moment. She had thought of leaving the car in plain view in the driveway to speak for itself, but in the end she had opted for hiding the evidence in the garage until she could find a gentle way to break it to him. Now she realized there was no such way.

"Dad—there's something I—uh—"

But his mind had already switched tracks. "Mmmm. What's that I smell? Dinner I hope—I'm starved."

"Katie left a pot roast in the oven," she said, relieved to be temporarily off the hook. "I'm supposed to take it out in twenty minutes."

Katie de Vries was their day housekeeper, a sturdy Dutch lady in her sixties who didn't seem to be bothered by Mr. Curtis's chauvinistic remarks, such as when he called her a "treasure" and asked why some man hadn't snatched her up years ago. She always laughed and said something like, "Go on, Mr. Curtis, if I were twenty years younger, you wouldn't stand a chance."

Actually, Patti also considered her dad's chauvinistic remarks fairly harmless. Like most of her friends' fathers, he just had a weird sense of humor. There was no getting around the fact that he was too conservative, but still she wouldn't want him to be like Gayle and Tracy's father, who played piano in a nightclub in Sacramento and wore lots of gold jewelry and clingy shirts. What really bothered Patti about her dad was that he could never seem to see her side of things. If she could accept him in spite of his being so old-fashioned, why couldn't he recognize that she wasn't a little girl anymore—that she was almost grown up, in fact? He didn't think she was capable of making any decisions on her own—even about something as small as doing her homework on the floor.

Patti decided to escape and scooped up the untidy sprawl of books and notepaper, then padded down the hallway to her bedroom at the far end of their modern ranch. Being alone in her bedroom always made Patti feel a little cut off from the rest of the world. She couldn't help thinking about all the times her mom used to come in and sit down on her bed to talk when Patti was feeling bad about something. After a while she would get up and smooth the bedspread flat again, just as effortlessly as she had smoothed over Patti's hurt.

But now she didn't mind being alone; it gave her a chance to sort out her feelings about Tim. Had she mistaken the way he looked at her that afternoon? Had touching her hand been just a meaningless gesture? She didn't think so—but then she'd had so little experience in those things. Perhaps she was reading too much into Tim's simply wanting her as a friend. Or maybe, she concluded, it was too soon for either of them to know how they really felt.

Patti sighed and flopped down on her bed. There was just no simple way to straighten out all the mixed-up feelings that were crowding her life at the moment.

Then she remembered about the piece of paper with Tim's number and fished around in her book bag to find it. She had never before believed in things like rabbits' feet and four-leaf clovers bringing people luck, but as she sat there, turning the paper over and over in her hand, she couldn't help but feel that it somehow brought her closer to Tim.

"You're not eating," said Mr. Curtis as he watched Patti pick at her food. "Not coming down with anything, are you?"

"I'm fine, Dad—really."

"What's bothering you then? Anything you want to tell me about?"

However much she complained about her father not understanding her, Patti couldn't help marveling at her father's constant concern for her.

She took a deep breath. *Here goes nothing.* "Dad—it's about the car." Without taking another breath, she plunged ahead. By the time she had finished, her father had stopped cutting his meat and was staring at her, frowning.

"You're absolutely positive this accident was your fault?" he asked after a long, heart-stopping silence. "Were there any witnesses?"

"No, but—"

He held up his fork to silence her. "If it happened as you described it, I'd have to say—as an insurance agent, not your father—that it doesn't appear to be a clear case of one hundred percent blame on either side."

She had been expecting anger, so his reaction took her completely by surprise. "But— but—I just told you, I wasn't looking where I was going!"

"Well, now, that means you're assuming this boy *was* looking. How much do you really know him, Patti? What kind of driving record does he have?"

Unthinkingly she blurted out, "He said he got a ticket last year, and that's why he couldn't get insurance, but I don't see what that has to do with—"

"No insurance!" Mr. Curtis echoed incredulously. "That settles it then. The boy is obviously irresponsible, as well as a negligent driver. As disappointed as I am in your carelessness, Patti, I can't let you shoulder all the blame for this. To be fair, I won't hold him responsible for the damage to my car, but you can be darn sure the company won't be paying for his."

"You can't do this!" Patti wailed, leaping out of her chair. "It was my fault. And Tim's been so nice about it. You just can't do this to him, Dad!"

Mr. Curtis's stern expression softened the tiniest bit, but he remained firm. "I can see you like this boy, and I'm sure he went out of his way to be charming after what happened.

But, Pattycake," he said, using an old endearment that made her cringe, "I've always thought you were too smart to be snowed by someone in a situation like this."

"You just don't understand at all!"

"I understand more than you think," he replied evenly. "After all, I happen to have been around a few more years than you. Now—why don't you give me this Tim's number? I'll call his parents and straighten it out with them."

Fifteen minutes later, having exhausted all her protests, Patti went tearfully to her room to get the phone number. She shoved it at her father as if it had suddenly sprouted a deadly fungus. *I hope he knows he's ruining my whole life.*

Frank Curtis disappeared into his den, where he made all his calls. When he emerged a short while later, he was shaking his head, the expression on his face a combination of outrage and disbelief.

"I don't believe it," he said slowly, shaking his head. "I just don't believe it."

"What happened?" Patti asked nervously, her heart beating fast and hard.

"I just spoke with Tim's mother. She's the one—the woman I was telling you about—the lady lawyer!"

Patti felt dizzy, as if she might faint. It can't be happening, she told herself. Coincidences like that just didn't happen to normal, everyday people living in Clinton, California. Her thoughts spun as if in a cyclone. Only one thing stood clear in the midst of it all: whatever slight chance she'd had with Tim was surely destroyed.

Chapter Four

"It couldn't be that bad," Denise argued. "Nothing could be *that* bad."

"You're right. It's worse than bad. Catastrophic. Maybe even cataclysmic."

"Cataclysmic?"

Patti slid her ten-speed into the bike rack at the upper end of the parking lot, then snapped the lock in place. In spite of everything, she was thankful that Denise was on one of her diet-and-exercise kicks so at least she wouldn't have to ride the three miles to and from school alone—at least not until Denise gave up on her diet.

"I just don't know how I can face Tim after last night," Patti said, moaning. "He must think I'm the world's biggest rat!"

"How do you know that? Give the guy a chance, will you? Besides, you didn't really do anything. It was your father mostly."

"My father's not the one who wrecked Tim's car."

"Well, I'm sure Tim knows you didn't do it on purpose. I mean, I know you were desperate to meet him, but you'd never go *that* far."

"Seriously, Denise, what am I going to do? What am I going to say when I see him?"

"I don't know. Do you have to see him? Maybe you could transfer to another school." Denise was struggling, unsuccessfully, not to smile.

"How about Anchorage, Alaska?" Patti replied glumly.

"What's in Anchorage?"

"I don't know—lots of snow, I guess. Maybe I could get myself a dog sled. Then I wouldn't ever have to drive another car."

"Yeah, but think of all those dogs you'd have to feed."

Patti looked at her in dismay. "This is just great. My life is falling apart, and my best friend is cracking dog jokes."

"Well, all I can say is, if this is all it takes to make your life fall apart, I'd hate to see you in a real crisis," Denise responded as they clomped up the worn slate steps of the main building. "Honestly, Patti, maybe all this is a blessing in disguise. Who knows how long it would have taken Tim to notice you otherwise?"

"Notice me! He's going to break out in hives whenever he hears my name after this!"

"C'mon, if he's as nice as you say, he'll take this whole thing in stride." Denise gave Patti a sheepish smile. "Actually, that's what my father said to me last night about Ms. Ketchum when I spilled hot chocolate all over my book report. He said there are worse things in life than Ernest Hemingway getting a cocoa mustache."

Patti giggled. "Like drinking hot chocolate when you're supposed to be on a diet, right?"

Denise groaned. "Why can't I learn to keep my mouth shut? And in more ways than one!"

They had barely reached their lockers when the first bell went off, clattering and clanging its way through the cavernous, lime-green corridors. Suddenly the lazy stream of students drifting by turned into a jostling, frenzied throng. Denise grabbed Patti's arm.

"Listen, I gotta go. But we got so involved talking about Tim, I forgot to tell you—Jamie called last night. He wanted to know if I'd go to the Spring Fling with him."

"That's terrific, Den! I guess I was being pretty selfish about my problem, but how could you forget to tell me a thing like that?"

She shrugged casually, but her beaming face was a dead giveaway. "I guess I knew how I'd feel if I were you. When you're miserable, the last thing in the world you want to hear is somebody else's good news."

"Well, miserable or not, I still think it's fantastic. What did you tell him?"

"That I had a date with Mick Jagger and couldn't make it. What do you think, dummy?"

"Sorry I asked. Have you decided what you're going to wear?"

"Hey, give me a chance. The dance is still three weeks away. Jamie said he wanted to ask me before someone else did. Can you imagine anyone being so sweet?"

"I don't see what's so sweet about it. There's no reason he shouldn't think you've got lots of boyfriends."

"Yeah, you can see them lining up for me every day at lunchtime," Denise said and laughed.

"Don't knock it. At least you're going to the dance."

"You'll probably get asked, too. There's still plenty of time." A mischievous gleam crept into her eyes. "Who knows? Maybe Tim will ask you."

"Ha, that's a laugh. Even if he didn't hate me—he probably has a date lined up."

"Don't be so sure. Anyway, the dance theme is Hawaiian luau, so you won't have to worry about any references to a car."

Denise scooted out of the way as Patti held up her loose leaf and threatened to throw it at her.

Patti had modern dance first period, which was part of the PE program. Never had she been less in the mood to "soar," as Ms. Vogelman put it, to the strains of *The Rite of Spring*. It was not that she hated dance itself—it was doing it that was the problem. To say she was klutzy was putting it mildly, Patti thought. For instance, at the end of a recent pantomime exercise, Sally Stromberger came up to Patti and asked quite seriously if she was supposed to be a puppy on a leash. Actually, Patti had been trying to imitate a hummingbird, but she kept that to herself after Sally's question and pretended she had guessed right. Ms. Vogelman awarded her a C+ for originality.

As the class sunk into deep knee bends, Maureen Corcoran brushed up against Patti and whispered, "Heard about how you snagged Tim the other day. Neat trick. Wish I'd thought of it."

Patti shot her a dirty look, and Maureen giggled. There was no chance for her to reply as Ms. Vogelman, looking like a purple sausage in her leotard, went twirling across the floor with everyone in hot pursuit. "Light-ly, girls, lightly-ly," she trilled. "We're butterflies in flight, not a herd of elephants. . . ."

Although Maureen's comment in dance and Eddie Talbot's announcement the day before in chemistry had given Patti some idea of how many people were finding out about the accident, it wasn't until she was peeling off her sweaty tights in the locker room that Patti discovered just how fast gossip really traveled at McKinley. It seemed everyone in the whole school had heard about the accident and thought of it as some huge joke.

"Nice going, Curtis," yelled Leona Hanson over the roar of the showers. "I hear you really socked it to Tim McBride!"

"I hope you know you've set back the cause of women drivers at least a hundred years!" Ella Preston cried militantly.

Patti bore all the teasing with good-natured embarrassment. But any hopes she'd had of the whole disastrous affair settling quietly were crushed as the bantering continued throughout the rest of the day. She sat through whispered wisecracks in English and in typing messed up a test, coming out with a score of eighteen words a minute after subtracting two points for each mistake. It was beginning to look as if she could do nothing right. By lunchtime she felt like a walking jinx.

"Maybe I should tape a big sign to my back: Beware of Klutz!" she complained to Denise and Tracy, who were sitting and sunning on McKinley's front lawn.

"How about Disaster in Progress?" suggested Tracy sweetly.

"Some help you guys are," Patti muttered. "I thought you were my friends."

"We are, we are!" they said in chorus.

"Have you run in—I mean, have you seen Tim yet?" Gayle asked, flopping down beside them on the grass.

Three-quarters of the student body could be seen sprawled across the spacious lawn in front of the school. It was much too nice to stay inside. The thermometer outside the gym read eighty-nine degrees, and a cloudless sky the color of well-faded denim sailed serenely overhead. On a day like that, Patti thought, she should be kicking up her heels instead of kicking herself. Worry had worked itself into a tight knot in the pit of her stomach, making her cheese-and-sprout sandwich taste like rubber between two pieces of dry bread.

Before she could answer Gayle's question,

Denise nudged her in the ribs. "Speak of the devil!" she whispered. "Don't look now, but someone you know is coming this way."

Patti whirled about to find a pair of familiar blue eyes gazing down at her. "Tim!" she almost screamed, swallowing hard to clear her throat of the bite of sandwich that was lodged firmly there. A surge of heat rushed up her neck. *Say something!* a voice inside her was shouting, but she couldn't think of a thing to say.

"Hi, Patti," Tim said, stuffing his hands self-consciously into his jean pockets.

Of all the things she'd lain awake the night before imagining he would say to her, "Hi, Patti," definitely wasn't one of them.

"Hi," she finally managed to spit out.

He started to say something, then glanced nervously over at her friends.

Denise took the hint right away. "We were just leaving, weren't we?" she piped up, jamming the remains of her lunch back into its bag and casting fierce looks at the twins. The three of them jumped to their feet almost in unison. "See ya, Patti!" they called, breaking into telltale giggles as they hurried off toward the cafeteria.

Patti wasn't sure being alone with Tim was better than having him yell at her in front of her friends. She sat there dumbly, struggling to find the words that would show Tim how sorry she was. But "sorry" wasn't going to fix his car, she knew. *My father stuck bamboo under my fingernails to make me give him your number*, she thought of saying as her desperation grew. No, he'd never believe it. What about the truth then? About how she'd tried to explain it to her dad, and somehow it had come out all wrong.

"Tim, I—"

"Wait a minute, Patti," Tim interrupted, dropping down beside her. "There's something I want to say first, so you can stop looking at me like I'm a policeman getting ready to arrest you. I know you didn't have anything to do with your father calling up last night."

"You do?"

He grinned. "Yeah, I'm not as dumb as I look. I figured you tried to tell your dad and it got blown out of proportion, right?"

Patti breathed a huge sigh of relief, then recounted the previous night's episode at the dinner table. "I've never seen him so determined! Once he'd made up his mind, that was it. He wouldn't even listen to me. And when he found out who your mother was—" she stopped in mid-sentence.

Tim nodded in sympathy. "It's like the song: 'immovable object' meets 'irresistible force.' "

Patti stared at him uncomprehendingly. "Huh?"

"Our parents," he said. "Looks like my mom has finally met her match. I didn't think there was another person on this planet as stubborn as she is."

"What did your mom say after my dad called?" she asked.

"She did a lot of hopping around and yelling at first. Then she calmed down and decided she was going to sue your dad's company for the money to fix the car."

Patti groaned. When Dad found out about this! "I can't believe it! It's like they're having some kind of personal war and using us as an excuse."

"Kind of looks that way, doesn't it?" He slouched back on his elbows, adjusting his faded orange visor against the glare of the noonday sun.

"I wish I had the money—I'd give it to you myself," she said. "Maybe I could pay you back when I get a summer job?"

"No way. You don't know my mom, anyway. Once she sinks her teeth into something like this, there's no letting go. You can bet she'll see this to the gruesome end."

"Well, she's in for some stiff competition then. My dad isn't known for giving up easily, either. He doesn't even think women should be lawyers in the first place. Isn't that awful?"

Tim stared at her for a few seconds, then they both burst out laughing.

"It's incredible," he said. "They're supposed to be the grown-ups, and they're acting like a couple of kids!"

"Hey, that's not fair," Patti argued. "*We're* kids, and look how reasonable we are."

"Let's face it. You and I are special—that's what comes of being only children."

"Do we have to give up?" Patti asked. "Isn't there something we could do to change their minds? There's got to be a better way of working this out than fighting about it."

"Tell you what," Tim suggested. "You work on your dad, and I'll see if I can't make a crack or two in Mom's armor. Meanwhile, I don't see why you and I can't be friends. Deal?" He stuck out his hand.

"Deal." His clasp sent tingles up her arm; but she was not prepared for the rush of sensation that overwhelmed her when he brushed her chin with the back of his other hand, tilting her head back to meet his gaze.

"I like you, Patti Curtis," he said. "Even if your driving isn't worth beans."

Chapter Five

Patti sailed away from school in a daze, unaware that the wheels of her ten-speed were touching the ground—until she hit a pothole that nearly caused her to lose her balance. After that she slowed down enough for Denise, who was pedaling furiously half a block behind, to catch up.

"Whew!" Denise sighed as she mopped her heat-flushed face with the sleeve of the sweatshirt that was knotted loosely over her shoulders. "You're not thinking of trying out for the Olympics by any chance?"

"I just want to get to my dad's office," Patti explained between breaths.

Denise looked puzzled. "Can't you talk to him at home?"

"I could, but it wouldn't be the same. I want this to be sort of like, um, a business call. I figured he might take me more seriously in more professional surroundings."

"I get it," said Denise with a knowing grin. "In other words, he can't yell at you if people are listening."

"You're something, Hodgekiss," Patti retorted. "You're the only person I know who could make Henry Kissinger feel like a Fuller Brush salesman."

They finally slowed down as they approached the welcome shade of downtown Clinton, swerving now and then to avoid getting drenched by a sprinkler. Clinton always reminded Patti a little of an oasis in the middle of a desert. Unlike many Central Valley towns, Clinton's founding fathers had spared nothing when it had come to planting trees and other assorted greenery. The result was that in the middle of heat spells, which regularly soared into the hundreds, their little town looked cool and inviting.

At that time of the year, the mock plum trees surrounding the town plaza were a solid cloud of pink. Tiny, fragrant petals fluttered in the girls' wakes as they turned onto Main Street, where most of the shops and businesses were clustered. Normally they would have stopped at Baskin-Robbins for an ice-cream cone, but since Patti was in a hurry and Denise on a diet, they bypassed it reluctantly. Patti could hear her friend's soft groan as they rode past the familiar pink polka-dot facade. Finally Patti braked to a stop in front of a small, rustic-looking building, surrounded on one side by the Bank of America and on the other by the Wee Care pet-grooming salon. The sign outside read: AGRI-GROWERS INSURANCE GROUP—FRANK CURTIS, AGENT.

"Call me when it's over," Denise called as she breezed past. "I'd rather not be around when the heads start rolling, if you don't mind!"

Patti shook a clenched fist in reply.

Mrs. Willet, her father's longtime secretary, looked up from her typewriter as Patti entered the air-conditioned reception office. Her plump, powdered cheeks lifted in a wide smile.

"What a nice surprise, Patti! I haven't seen you in ages." She wagged a playful finger. "I suppose it's a boyfriend who's taking up all your time now."

Patti blushed. "Not exactly."

Absently Mrs. Willet patted her immaculate, sprayed silver coif. "Well, never you mind, dear. One of these days a nice boy will come along, and he'll make all the waiting worthwhile."

Maybe he already has, Patti told herself.

Then again, maybe not. Tim had said he liked her, nothing more. Liking someone didn't necessarily mean instant romance. *Go slowly, Patti Curtis, don't let your emotions run away with you.*

"Is my father busy?" she asked the secretary.

"On the phone," she replied. "But go ahead in. I'm sure he won't mind your waiting inside so long as you're quiet."

No sooner had Patti tiptoed into the wood-paneled inner office than she realized she couldn't have chosen a worse moment to make her appearance. Frank Curtis sat hunched over the phone, his face an ominous dark red. He was speaking loudly—the loudest a person can get without actually shouting—to whomever was on the other end.

"You can sue me all the way to the Supreme Court for all I care!" he barked into the receiver. "That doesn't change the facts one iota. If that irresponsible son of yours—yes, that's right, *irresponsible*—was such a good driver, why couldn't he get insurance in the first place?"

Patti slunk down in her chair. She didn't have to be a genius to guess it was Tim's mother he was talking to.

"Well, if you ask me—what that boy needs is a good talking to by his father!"

Pause.

"Hrrmph! There's no need to get insulted. I'm sure your marital affairs are no business of m—"

Pause.

"Not *that* kind of affairs. Now just hold on a minute, I didn't mean to imply—" His expression blackened. "Slander? You can't sue me for slander! I never—"

There was the sound of the dial tone, and Mr. Curtis stared at the receiver for a bewildered, furious moment before slamming it down. For the first time he took notice of Patti, slumped miserably in a chair. Slowly a sheepish grin began to steal over his stormy features.

"Guess I kind of got carried away, huh?" he said. "I've never known a woman who could get under my skin the way that one can, though. Stubborn as a mule!"

Patti cleared her throat, smiling weakly. "Sounds a little like you, Dad."

He chuckled softly. "Well—maybe. But a man has to stand his ground these days—the way you gals take advantage."

"Ugh!" She rolled her eyes to the ceiling. "I don't see how Tim's mother can be all bad. She did a pretty good job raising Tim."

His brows shot up. "And what would you

know about that, young lady? I hope you haven't been hanging around with this boy—he's trouble, don't kid yourself about that."

"Oh, Daddy, you act like he's some kind of juvenile delinquent. I promise you, he's nothing like that at all. He's really nice. If you could only meet him—"

"Spare me the honor," he said. "One McBride is about all I can handle at the moment."

"But—"

"And I don't want you hanging around with that character, either. Understood?"

"But, Dad—that's so unfair!" Patti was dangerously close to tears.

Mr. Curtis heaved his solid frame from his chair and came around to place his arm affectionately about his daughter's shoulders.

"Look, Pattycake, I know things haven't been all that easy since Mom—" He paused, as if unsure whether or not the water he was treading was too deep. "I'm not saying I'm such a perfect parent, but I do know a few things in spite of my ancient ideas. So trust me on this, OK?"

Patti's throat was so tight that all she could manage was a nod, even though she wanted to disagree.

"Now what was so urgent that you couldn't wait to tell me until I got home?" he asked.

She bit her lip. "Nothing, Dad," she lied. "I—I just wanted to stop in and say hi, that's all."

"In that case, what do you say we sneak down to the ice-cream parlor for one of those butterscotch sundaes you're so crazy about?"

Stop treating me like I'm a little kid! she felt like shouting. When she was five years old and scraped her knees, her father bought her ice cream. Nothing had changed, at least as far as he was concerned.

"Some other time, OK?" she mumbled. "I've got a ton of homework."

He shrugged, trying not to look hurt. "Sure, Pattycake. We'll go another time."

Patti fled quickly outside so he wouldn't see that she was crying.

"Goodness! I haven't seen such a long face since that boyfriend of yours moved to Philadelphia," said Mrs. de Vries, pausing in the midst of mopping the kitchen floor to peer at Patti over the tops of her spectacles.

"Oh, Katie, that was two whole years ago. And Tommy Leidecker wasn't my boyfriend. We were just friends—he never even kissed me." Actually, he tried once, but she was wearing braces at the time and had a morbid fear of cutting his lips.

61

The stout housekeeper tapped the side of her head. "Ha! I knew it. That's what's behind this face of yours—a boy."

Katie de Vries fancied herself something of a mind reader. She also believed that almost every sickness known to mankind could be cured with one of her herbal teas. Patti loved Mrs. de Vries and regarded her as a part-time grandmother.

"No—yes—sort of," she confessed. "It's complicated."

"Well, why don't you come over here and try explaining it then? Never mind about the floor. Sit down and I'll make you a nice cup of comfrey tea." She winked. "Good for the nerves."

Patti smiled. Comfrey. It sounded as if she were going to be wrapped up in a big fluffy quilt and maybe have a bedtime story read aloud to her—which didn't seem like such a terrible idea at the moment. Why was it she couldn't even make up her mind whether she was still a little kid or an almost-adult? She planted her elbows on the table and nibbled gloomily at the slice of raisin bread Katie had set down in front of her.

"This wouldn't have anything to do with the boy who smashed into your father's car, by any chance, would it?" probed Katie, settling into the chair opposite Patti.

"How did you know about that?" Patti stared incredulously into Katie's flushed, sturdy face, framed by an ivory halo of curls.

Mrs. de Vries laughed. "No trick to it this time. Your father was complaining so loudly at breakfast, I wouldn't be surprised if half the neighborhood heard."

"Well, anyway, it wasn't Tim's fault. *I* ran into him. Not on purpose, of course. But Dad won't believe me. I guess it's easier to blame some stranger than your own daughter."

"Now, Patti, you know your father's not that kind of person," she scolded gently. "Right or wrong, I'm sure he has his reasons for believing what he does."

"But if they are the wrong reasons, what difference does it make? Either way, Tim loses out. And I know he'll end up hating me even if he doesn't now." Fresh tears shimmered briefly in her eyes before she brushed them away with an angry fist.

"Ah!" Katie's brows arched upward. "Now I'm beginning to see. What you're really concerned about are Tim's feelings for you, no?"

Patti gulped and nodded. "It's so unfair. I just know Dad wouldn't be this way about Tim if he could only meet him and see how nice he is."

"Perhaps." Katie smiled, a faraway look in

her blue eyes. "But you must try and understand your father's feelings, too, Patti dear."

"What's there to understand?"

"Patti, Patti—you've grown into such a pretty girl. Your father sees how attracted you are to this boy, and maybe he's just a tiny bit afraid."

"Afraid?" she echoed. "Of what?"

Katie's large, competent hand patted her arm. "Of the future, Patti. You don't have to be a mind reader to see that!"

Chapter Six

Monday mornings, on the way to school, Patti always stopped to have breakfast at Denise's. It had become a kind of tradition. She didn't know exactly how it started, except it had to do with the fact that Mrs. Hodgekiss volunteered at a convalescent home Sunday mornings, so she always cooked something extra special on Monday to make up for it. That morning it was waffles with strawberries and whipped cream.

"I could eat a mountain of these," said Patti as she put a forkful into her mouth.

Denise shot her a pained look over a bowl of strawberries, plain with no cream. "Ugh! Do you know how many calories there are in one waffle, not to mention the cream?"

Mrs. Hodgekiss plopped another waffle onto Patti's plate. She was a fair-haired, plumper version of her daughter, with the same pretty, lightly freckled face.

"Here we go again!" She laughed. "Denise has turned into a walking calorie computer since we went shopping for a dress for the dance."

"Would you believe there was nothing, absolutely zilch, in anything but sizes seven and nine?" Denise moaned.

Patti, who was a size seven, suggested, "You could always make your own dress. Didn't you get an A in home ec last semester?"

"That was for my lasagna Bolognese. The last dress I made I sewed the zipper in backward and had to rip the whole thing apart when I was done."

"Yeah, I remember that lasagna," piped in Lonnie, Denise's ten-year-old brother. "Skipper ate some and got sick all over the rug."

At the sound of his name, Skipper raised his big shaggy white head off his paws, blinked at them, and then went back to sleep. From his cage by the window, Rico squawked, "Skipper! Skipper! You lazy dog! Skipper!"—a performance the sheep dog ignored completely.

"Gross!" yelled seven-year-old Stacey. One of her braids had slipped unnoticed into the whipped cream on her plate, and Patti reached over to rescue it. Thirteen-year-old Pam started to giggle uncontrollably, prompting the baby to bang his spoon delightedly against his high chair.

"Hey, settle down, gang," grunted Mr. Hodgekiss good-naturedly, hunching his burly shoulders over his plate. "Mind if I eat my breakfast in peace?"

"Peace?" echoed his wife, grinning. "My goodness, if we ever had a peaceful meal in this house, we wouldn't know how to eat it."

Patti thought automatically of the meals she shared at home with her dad, which, although companionable, seldom got noisier than "pass the salt, please" or "sure you wouldn't like another dab of the potato salad?" The last two days had been even worse. Since Friday, a kind of undeclared pact of silence had existed between them. Nothing on the surface, of course. If anything, they were both being extra polite to each other, but inside, Patti's resentment boiled.

To top everything off, Tim hadn't even called, although he'd half-promised he would. She didn't really blame him, but that didn't make it any easier. The phone had been deathly silent all weekend except for Denise calling to fill her in on the latest with Jamie and her diet. She'd lost five pounds so far. Terrific, thought Patti.

That morning she'd woken up with an uneasy feeling that Monday wasn't going to be much better. It was just a vague notion at first as she fought her way up through the layers of sleep. Then she remembered. Monday was the day she was going to try out for the a cappella choir. Mrs. Jaffe had arranged it with Mr. Reese after Patti finally decided Denise was right about taking chances. What did she have to lose, after all? And if she did get in, it would mean extra time she could spend with Tim—time her father couldn't object to if he found out. It was very tempting. But there were still too many ifs. *If* Mr. Reese liked her. *If* she didn't blow it with Tim. If, if, if . . .

If only I had laryngitis right now, she wished half seriously. *Then I wouldn't have to worry about it.*

As if reading her thoughts, Denise remarked, "Patti's trying out for the a cappella choir today. Isn't that neat? I'll bet she's a shoo-in."

Lonnie perked up. "How much d'you wanna bet? I've got three dollars saved from my birthday."

"Not *that* kind of bet, dummy," Denise shot back disgustedly. "How can anyone be so stupid!"

"Stupid!" parroted Rico, causing everyone to break up, including Mr. Hodgekiss.

"Hark, the natives grow restless," observed Nadine coolly as she speared a tidy forkful of waffle. She was the oldest at seventeen and a half, also somewhat of a snob in Denise's opinion, who claimed the only things her sister cared about were her collection of Squeeze albums and the gold necklace her boyfriend had given her before he went away to college.

"I was in the choir at my school," Denise's mother recalled wistfully, wiping a stray hair from her forehead. "We sure had a lot of fun— even put on a couple of operettas."

"Mom, I didn't know you could sing," Denise responded in astonishment.

She waved her spatula at them. "There's a lot kids don't know about their parents. And it wouldn't hurt them one little bit to find out!"

"Good luck, Patti," called Mr. Hodgekiss cheerily as she and Denise got up from the table to leave for school.

For some reason, the younger children found this hilarious, and when Patti gave a last glance over her shoulder, they were doubled up over their plates in hysterics.

"Sometimes," Denise said, rolling her eyes

dramatically, "I think how nice it would be if I lived on the moon."

Patti smiled. "What about Jamie? Wouldn't it get lonely up there after a while?"

"I'll let you know after I've met the man in the moon," she wisecracked. "What if he looks like Rick Springfield?"

Patti giggled, already feeling a lot better about facing the day.

That afternoon, as she stood in front of Mr. Reese and the whole a cappella choir, she wasn't so sure. Anxiously she scanned their faces. Gayle caught her eye with a little half-wave of encouragement. Tim offered a smile, which warmed her in spite of her cold feet and churning stomach.

Patti licked her lips and glanced over at Mr. Reese, who sat perched on the piano stool like an elderly ostrich, his spindly neck thrust forward, peering at the sheet music in front of him. Patti had chosen a selection from *The Magic Flute*, a piece she had sung dozens of times without any problems. But at that moment, the inside of her mouth felt like Kleenex, and she was sure she wouldn't remember a single word.

But as Mr. Reese began banging away enthusiastically on the piano, the music she knew so well swelled effortlessly from her throat. She forgot how self-conscious she'd been a minute before.

The notes rose and fell, enclosing her in her own private bubble—the way it was whenever she sang alone. She could almost have believed, if she closed her eyes, that she was back in her little tree-cave by the creek.

Suddenly she knew it was going to be all right. No matter what happened—if she was accepted or not—everything was going to be OK. Tim's presence stretched toward her like an invisible tide, filling her with warmth and joy. She drew a deep breath and sent the final notes soaring upward with more emotion than she had ever sung before.

There was an instant of silence, then the choir members exploded in applause. Gayle rocketed from her seat, clapping wildly while Tim issued several earsplitting hurrahs. Patti didn't quite know how to react. She stood there awkwardly, a grin plastered in place, then gave a little bow.

"Very nice, Miss Curtis," intoned Mr. Reese, his thin lips stretching into a smile. "Very nice indeed." He sounded surprised, as if wondering where she had been hiding all this time.

After Mr. Reese spoke, Patti, feeling both happy and relieved, darted out of the room.

"You were fan-tas-tic!" Tim said and whooped, catching her up in a bear hug of congratulations. "Didn't I tell you you would be?"

Patti noticed several people staring at them, probably wondering if they were an item. She flushed, thinking, *Let them wonder.* "You really think Mr. Reese liked me?" she asked.

"Like you? Hey, are you kidding? He probably would have asked for your autograph if you hadn't run off like that."

"Ha!" she exclaimed.

"Seriously," Tim said. "You were sensational, and you know it. I don't know why I'm telling you all this. Pretty soon your head'll be so big they'll have to make all the doors around here wider to let you through."

Patti giggled. "Well, at least that's better than melting into a big puddle, like I thought I was going to."

He took her hand as they strolled across the patio, heading for the paths that branched among the acacias. Patti felt the thrill of his touch travel up her arm like a mild electric shock. She caught the faint whiff of a spicy aftershave and noticed how the hair along his forearm was tinted with light gold. Part of her felt as if it were the most natural thing in the world to be walking hand in hand with him, while another part of her felt as though she were walking through a magical dream. Later, when she was alone, she knew she would remember every single detail of that moment.

"I wonder when Mr. Reese will let me know his decision," she said.

"I'm sure he's already made it. But he'll want to talk to Mrs. Jaffe first. Don't worry, you'll probably know by tomorrow or the day after."

"I just hope I can hold my breath that long."

"You're in," Tim assured her.

Patti couldn't seem to stop grinning. "I can't believe I did it. I actually got up in front of everyone and sang. Even if I don't make the choir, I feel like I've just climbed a mountain or something."

He stopped and looked at her. "You know what this could mean, don't you? If we're in the choir together—what with the spring concert rehearsals and all—maybe our parents'll have to think twice about keeping up with this crazy feud."

Patti's soaring heart landed with a thud inside her chest. "I don't know, Tim. I've never seen my father so dead set on anything. He—he even told me not to see you."

"You, too? Wow, and I thought I was the only one. Mom landed on me with both feet about this. I'm embarrassed to tell you what she said about you."

"It couldn't be worse than what my dad said about you."

"Yeah? I can guess. He thinks I'm a juvenile delinquent, right? Mom said you were just a little gold digger and that I should keep away from you or sew my pockets shut."

"Me?" Patti's face burned at the thought.

Tim walked around her, pretending to examine her with great interest. "Hmmm, yes, very interesting."

"What on earth are you doing?" Patti cried indignantly, swinging around to face him.

He grinned. "Looking for your horns and tail."

"You rat! I'll get you for that!"

"Oh yeah, what did you have in mind?" Abruptly he drew her against him and kissed her lightly on the mouth. Patti felt warm and prickly, as if it were the first time she had ever been kissed. In a way, it was.

"Nothing that drastic," she said lightly, not wanting him to see how deeply affected she was. Why, her insides were quivering!

They walked a little farther in silence before Tim blurted, "Any chance you could talk your dad into letting me take you to the Spring Fling?"

Patt' was stunned. In spite of everything that had happened, she still couldn't believe Tim McBride was actually asking her to the dance.

"I—I don't know," she answered honestly. "I'll try."

Try was putting it mildly, she thought. If there was a chance in the world of changing her father's mind, she would do everything she could to find it. Didn't they say that all was fair in love and war? Well, she was in love . . . and this was war!

Chapter Seven

"I can't believe it." Patti wandered from the music room in a daze, while Gayle thumped her on the back excitedly. Denise caught up with them in the hallway, giving a loud scream when Patti announced, "I'm in."

"And that's not all," gushed Gayle. "Mr. Reese wants her to do a solo for the spring concert!"

"Wow," shrieked Denise, "if they put it on TV, you'll be a star!"

"Wait until your father hears this," said Gayle. "He'll forget all about the accident." She thumped Patti's back one more time before rushing off to her next class.

"I feel dizzy," Patti said, clutching Denise's arm.

"You're hyperventilating," Denise assured her knowingly. "Nadine gets that way all the time from blowing on her nails to make them dry faster. Just calm down before you faint or something."

"I can't calm down!"

"Well, don't worry. If you faint I'll get Tim to give you mouth-to-mouth resuscitation."

"Now that's an idea." Patti laughed as the bell sounded its summons.

Denise lowered her voice to a whisper. "Have you told Tim the bad news about the dance yet?"

Instantly Patti sobered, remembering her father's reaction two nights before, when she had timidly broached the subject of the dance.

"Absolutely not!" he had bellowed. "And that's the last I want to hear of it."

Patti took a deep breath and plunged ahead anyway. "Dad, if you're worried about Tim's driving, I've already worked it out with Denise, and she says we can double with her and Jamie."

"Sounds like you've been doing quite a bit of planning without my go-ahead," he observed coolly. "Don't you think you should have asked me first before you worked it all out with Denise?"

"But you would have said no!"

"Darn right. I won't have you running around with troublemakers. There are plenty of nice boys for you to go to the dance with."

"But Tim *is* nice," she protested, knowing it was useless to argue but still unable to stop herself. "Besides, no one else has asked me."

"And they're not going to if they see you mooning over Tim," he pronounced emphatically.

Patti felt herself growing desperate. "If you could only talk to him—"

"I don't have to talk to him to know what he is. Just look at the statistics! One moving violation and one accident in less than a year of driving—without insurance, I might add. And he comes from a broken home with no father to provide guidance and a crazy mother in trousers who won't listen to reason." Frank Curtis, insurance agent, was big on statistics.

Look who's talking! Patti felt like yelling. As far as she was concerned, her father and Tim's mother were two of a kind. She might as well try to convince one of the carved heads on Mount Rushmore! Why did it always have to be that way between her and her father? Her mom had always been able to reason with him, she thought. Her mom had been gentle, wise, and had had a sense of humor that was always evident even when she was keeping a straight face. Why couldn't she be more like her mother? Patti agonized. Her dad had respected her mom, so he had listened to her. He couldn't respect Patti, because he thought of her as a baby. Patti longed for a way to show him how mature, sensible, and grown-up she was.

Instead, she burst into tears. "I'll die if I can't go to the dance with Tim!" Sobbing, she ran down the hall to lock herself in the bathroom for what turned out to be the longest shower she had taken in years. . . .

Patti was annoyed with Denise for having pricked her bubble. "You would have to bring that up. No, I haven't told Tim—and I'm not going to. The dance is still two weeks away."

"Yeah, maybe your dad will change his mind," Denise suggested hopefully.

Patti's frown deepened. "Sure, and maybe it'll snow by lunchtime."

"You never know." Peering into her locker, Denise unearthed a pair of grungy, crumpled-up gym socks. She held them aloft and grinned triumphantly. "See, I even have my mittens handy just in case!"

For some reason, that didn't surprise Patti one bit.

Patti had just settled into the seat Tim had saved for her when Mr. Reese began passing out mimeographed scores of the pieces they would be performing in the spring concert.

"As you can see," he said in his rich baritone, "we have our work cut out for the next few weeks. I'll be posting a list of rehearsal times on the bulletin board tomorrow, and I want every one of you"—his eyes, under their shaggy shelf of eyebrow, swept the room imperiously—"to arrange your schedules accordingly. Understood?"

A ripple of assent swept the room.

"Some of you may have heard a rumor that the concert is to be televised," he continued. "Well . . ." he paused, smiling, while they all waited in suspense, barely breathing.

"Sadist!" muttered Gabe North, a freckle-faced boy who sat behind Patti. She recognized him as the president of the Humanities Club.

"I spoke with the people at KPUX this morning, and they tell me . . ." another silence, accompanied by a smile.

"I can't stand it!" said Martha Beal. "What did they say?"

Mr. Reese cleared his throat. "It's on. They've scheduled a camera crew to be here on the twenty-ninth. What do you say? Think we'll be ready for them?"

A chorus of enthusiastic cries was their deafening response.

"OK, then, let's get down to business. We'll be doing a mixture of classical and pop pieces. An Elizabethan madrigal right on up to 'Oh Happy Day!' The longest, trickiest piece will be Mendelssohn's *Elijah*. I want you to study it thoroughly before we start rehearsing on Tuesday. The library has the record—first come, first serve. Otherwise, we'll be listening to my tape next week . . ."

As he rattled on, Patti was struck by the realization that the concert was less than four weeks away. Would she be ready by then? She was a novice, and the rest of the group was used to learning difficult music quickly. Panic nibbled at her insides.

Tim must have noticed how edgy she looked, for he murmured reassuringly, "Relax, Curtis, you'll do just fine. You'll be surprised how easy it is once you get into the swing of it."

She grimaced. "That's what my driver's ed instructor told me."

"I guess you can't win 'em all." He shrugged.

Patti glanced up to find Mr. Reese glowering at them. "When you two get through chatting, do you think we could get some work done?" he asked.

"Sorry, Mr. Reese, I'm all yours," Tim replied unabashedly. As soon as the teacher wasn't looking, he gave Patti a big wink.

Happiness flooded through her. She knew she would have to tell Tim about the dance sooner or later, but right now all she wanted to think about was how happy she was sitting next to him.

"What you need is a plan of action," counseled Denise as they sat licking their ice-cream cones at a tiny, glass-topped table in Baskin-Robbins, where they had stopped on their way home from school.

Denise was celebrating the fact that she had lost seven pounds by indulging in a double-decker rocky road and Jamoca almond fudge. Patti was consoling herself with rum pecan, because Tim had asked her to go to Baskin-Robbins with him first, and she'd had to turn him down. It was too close to her dad's office, and someone who knew him was bound to see them together. That was the trouble with small towns, she thought. Everybody knew everybody else, so if she and Tim started sneaking around behind their parents' backs, they would have about as much chance of not getting noticed as a police raid on the local health club.

"What kind of plan?" asked Patti suspiciously.

"A way for you and Tim to go to the dance—what else?"

"Forget it. I've tried every trick I know on Dad. He's not budging."

"Who said anything about budging?"

"If you're suggesting anything sneaky, you can forget that, too. I'd never get away with it."

Denise sighed at Patti's thickheadedness. "That's why you need a plan, silly."

"And I suppose you just happen to have one all figured out, right?"

"Naturally." Denise caught the last melting drops of ice cream with an expert flick of her tongue. "Oh, don't you see, Patti? It's really so romantic. Kind of like Romeo and Juliet."

"I hope that doesn't mean we have to end up killing ourselves," Patti said, sighing.

Denise giggled. "Nothing that drastic, I promise. Actually, I was thinking you could use a front."

"A what?"

"A front. You know, someone who pretends to be someone else. Like in that movie *The Sting*."

"You want me to sting my father?" Patti asked incredulously.

"In a manner of speaking. What you could do is pretend someone else was taking you to the dance—for a small fee this person might even be willing to pick you up at your house."

"OK, Den, who is he?" Patti asked suspiciously.

"Jamie's little brother."

"You've got to be kidding! *He's a freshman.*"

"So? Your dad doesn't have to know that."

"He's also only about four feet tall!"

Denise was beginning to wilt. "Well—you could always say he has retarded glands."

Suddenly they were both doubled up over the table. Janet Green and Billy Sanchez, who were sitting beside them, looked over at them as if they were crazy.

"I guess I didn't really think it out," Denise admitted when she finally regained her breath.

"If you mean the part about Jamie's little brother—you can say that again," Patti agreed. "But the stuff about having a plan wasn't half bad. I'll have to think about it—maybe I can come up with something."

An hour after leaving Denise, Patti was sprawled on her bed engrossed in a *Reader's Digest* article entitled "Teen Survival in the Eighties" when the phone rang. It was Tim.

"Is the coast clear?" he asked. When she told him her father was still at work, he breathed a sigh of relief. "Good. I was hoping

I wouldn't have to wear my Groucho Marx disguise when I come by to pick you up in a few minutes."

"Pick me up? What are you talking about? My dad would kill me."

"Look, Patti, I know how you feel about doing stuff behind his back. Believe me, I wouldn't ask if it wasn't important. More important than me, that is," he added playfully.

"Tim, you *are* important." She was glad he couldn't see her redden.

"So are you, Patti," he replied in a husky voice. "This whole thing is so stupid. Why do we have to sneak around like a couple of criminals, anyway? It's not like we're doing anything wrong. Oh, forget it—it was a dumb idea for me to call." He sounded frustrated, and she was afraid he'd hang up.

"No, Tim, wait. Where—where did you want to go?"

"Just over to Harry Purcell's house—you know him, he's in the choir. Anyway, Harry's got a recording of *Elijah*—you'd really flip if you could hear it on the stereo system his dad's got hooked up." He paused. "Besides all that, I wanted to be with you."

"What should I tell my dad?" she asked, chewing absently at her thumbnail. She really wanted to go, but she hated the thought of lying.

"Don't tell him anything. He's not there, so just leave a note. Tell him the truth—only scratch the part about who you're going with."

"I—I guess I could," she agreed slowly, torn between lying and her longing to be with Tim.

"I'll pick you up in fifteen minutes—now that I've got insurance," he said.

When they arrived a short while later, they found Harry's living room crowded with kids from the choir. Patti still felt a little awkward around the group, but that faded as she was greeted warmly by everyone there, and Gabe North moved over to make room for her on the couch. Harry brought them Cokes and passed around a bowl of potato chips.

Tim had been right about the stereo system. The sound coming out of the speakers was extremely strong and clear. The system itself was ultramodern, and the components— the speakers, turntable, and amplifier—were amazingly small. Harry's father, she learned, owned Good Vibes, Clinton's largest stereo-TV store, which gave him access to all the latest equipment. Patti closed her eyes and let the music wash over her. The thought of singing it herself on TV gave her goose bumps.

When it was over, someone put on a Donna Summer album. A throbbing disco beat pulsed from the compact speakers, and before long the living room floor was jammed with gyrating couples. Tim grabbed Patti's hand. "Come on," he yelled over the noise, "let's go somewhere quiet!"

He took her to Good Time Charlie's, a place downtown where they could talk and wouldn't be too conspicuous. They chose a dark booth near the back, and Tim ordered cheeseburgers and fries for both of them.

"Sorry you came?" he asked, his hand curling over hers on the tabletop.

Patti smiled. "I was just thinking that I wish it could be like this all the time. I really had fun, Tim."

"You mean you don't feel guilty anymore?"

"Well—I didn't exactly say that. I just hope my father doesn't find out, that's all." She darted a glance over her shoulder as if she expected to see her father pop up from the next booth at any moment.

"Watch out—there are spies everywhere," Tim whispered in a Russian accent, hoping to sound sinister.

Her laughter died suddenly as she saw the well-dressed, middle-aged woman who slid into the adjoining booth.

Patti nearly choked on a french fry. "Oh, my God—that's Mrs. Willet," she whispered. "She's my dad's secretary! What am I going to do?"

Tim lowered his voice. "Relax. She didn't see you, did she?"

She slumped down until her chin was almost level with the tabletop. Mrs. Willet had disappeared from view except for a wave of silver cresting the top of the adjoining booth. They were safe right then—but not for long. In order to get to the door, they would have to walk right by her.

Patti felt her excitement turn to a sour lump in the pit of her stomach. "I should've known something like this would happen," she said sadly.

"Don't panic," Tim said. "We haven't blown our cover yet." He motioned the waitress over and in his most charming desperate whisper asked, "Is there another way out of here?"

The girl, who wasn't much older than they, looked both flustered and pleased to be included in the intrigue. "There's a fire exit by the kitchen," she told them. "I'm really not supposed to let anyone use it, but—"

"It's a matter of life and death," Tim urged.

"I guess it would be OK." She winked. "Just this once."

Patti and Tim were outside in a flash. Not until they reached his car, parked across the street, did Patti collapse to catch her breath. Tim wrapped his arms around her, hugging her tightly.

"That was a close call," he said, kissing the top of her head, then bringing his lips down to nuzzle her cheek. "I guess I wasn't really thinking when I talked you into coming."

"It's not your fault, Tim. I could have stayed home if I'd really wanted to." At that moment, encircled in his arms and glowing with the warmth of his kisses, she was glad she hadn't.

He tipped her chin back so that her eyes met his searching gaze. "You're not just saying that to make me feel better?"

"Really, Tim," she murmured, her fingers playing with the golden curls that hung over the back of his collar, "I'm not sorry."

Liar, she was telling herself at the same time, *I'd be plenty sorry if Mrs. Willet had spotted me.*

Next time she had a feeling she wouldn't be so lucky.

Chapter Eight

By the end of the next week, rehearsals were in full swing. And when the choir wasn't rehearsing, Mr. Reese kept them busy with a whirl of related activities, such as picture-taking sessions for the school and town newspapers and getting measured for new choir robes. Patti and Tim were thrown together so much of the time at school that she forgot to be miserable about the time they couldn't spend together outside it. They had even devised a system where she could call him from Denise's, pretending to be Denise if his mother answered. Actually, Ann McBride sounded so nice, it was hard to believe she was the ogre her dad had painted her to be.

It wasn't until a week before the dance, when Patti went with Denise to try on dresses at Tracy and Gayle's, that a feeling of gloom set in. She'd have to come up with a plan soon, or she wouldn't be going to the dance. And it would have to be foolproof—she didn't want any near misses like the last time. Fortunately, Tracy had an idea.

"Why not come with me?" she suggested. "There're plenty of kids going stag. That way you're not really lying to your dad when you tell him you don't have a date with Tim."

"And no one's looking over your shoulder to see who you dance with!" supplied Denise. "Brilliant, my dear Tracy. Why didn't I think of it? It's so simple, it's perfect."

"That's probably why you didn't think of it," said Patti. "You were too busy plotting the big sting. Maybe you figured you could get Robert Redford to pose as my date."

Denise gave her a disgusted look. "No way— he's too old."

"Well, at least he's the right height." She told Tracy and Gayle about Denise's plan for her to go to the dance with Jamie's brother, which sent them all into gales of laughter.

The four of them spent the afternoon clustered around the full-length mirror in the twins' bedroom, trying on and discarding dresses. Gayle was going to the dance with Sandy Bostwick, the skateboard champ of McKinley, and had complained to her father that she hadn't a single thing to wear. The result was that the twins' father had brought home an armload of evening gowns borrowed from the singer who worked at the nightclub with him.

"How about this one?" asked Gayle, twirling before the mirror in a slinky gown that looked as if the entire Milky Way had been sewn onto it.

"It looks like something Cher would wear," commented her twin.

"Sandy would take one look at you and probably be blinded for life," said Denise.

"He could always wear sunglasses," Patti suggested jokingly. "Then everyone would think you were two movie stars." She rummaged through the pile of dresses, picking out a peach-colored voile with a full skirt and spaghetti straps. "This would look good on you, Gayle. It goes with your coloring."

Gayle struggled out of the one she was wearing and slipped the new one over her head. She gazed at her reflection for a long appraising moment, then uttered a deep sigh of satisfaction. "Perfect," she declared. They all agreed it was.

Tracy settled on a long, full skirt to go with a white silk blouse she already had. Patti and Denise continued trying things on just for the fun of it—Denise had already purchased a light blue silk jersey earlier in the week. She was down to a size nine.

Patti wondered if she should buy a new dress; she still wasn't one hundred percent sure she was going. What if her dad saw through her plan to go without a date? Somehow, though, she didn't think he would. Lately, he had been encouraging her to go out more—probably because he felt guilty about Tim. *I'll bet he'd fall all over himself to say yes if some other boy asked me*, she thought resentfully.

And the funny thing was that ever since she had gotten involved with the choir, it seemed other boys *were* paying more attention to her. She didn't know whether it was because she was meeting so many new people or because most of the time she was so busy and involved she forgot she'd ever thought of herself as shy and awkward.

Gabe North had asked her to a party his club was sponsoring for a new exchange student from Japan. Patti had almost accepted, until she realized he was asking her to be his date as well. Later, when she mentioned it to Tim, thinking he wouldn't mind knowing she had turned Gabe down, he surprised her by acting jealous.

"You'd probably be better off with Gabe,"

he'd said glumly. "At least you wouldn't have to sneak around with him."

Patti had been too upset to reply. That was why the dance was so important, she thought. It was an opportunity to convince Tim that he was the one she wanted to be with.

"Come on," urged Tracy, who had changed back into jeans and a T-shirt. "Let's get over to the mall before it closes. Macy's is giving free makeup lessons. If we hurry we can make it."

Patti struggled to take off a slinky black satin Mae West number. "Gosh!" she cried. "I never knew being gorgeous was so much work."

"Don't worry," Denise said, propelling her out the door. "Tim will appreciate it."

"There!" Katie de Vries put the finishing touches on Patti's upsweep and gave it a light spritz with the hair spray bottle. "If you're not the most beautiful girl at the dance, I'm turning in my fairy godmother's wand."

Patti hugged the stout housekeeper. "Thanks, Katie. I don't know how I would have managed without you."

The previous week, after her father had given his permission for her to go to the dance with Tracy, she had spent every extra minute looking for *the* dress to wear. She knew exactly what style she wanted, but none of the stores in Clinton had anything that came close, and it was too late to drive all the way into Sacramento. Finally, in desperation she consulted the pattern books at Fabric Corner and found what she was looking for there. Katie had volunteered to make the dress, knowing how busy Patti was with rehearsals. At the last minute she even insisted on doing Patti's hair.

Now Patti stood before the antique cheval mirror in her bedroom, marveling at the transformation. She had aimed for a look of classic simplicity with a pure white, Grecian-style dress that fell in soft folds to her knees. The dress was nipped in at the waist by a thin gold belt. The effect was stunning, showing off the natural olive tones in her skin and accentuating her slender curves. Gold hoop earrings and a pair of thin-strapped, gold, high-heeled sandals completed the picture of elegance.

"You'll have those boys falling all over themselves for a dance," Katie warned, waggling a finger at her. "Just be sure you don't break too many hearts tonight."

"No more than I can help," Patti quipped, thinking of Tim. Katie didn't know that Tim was the only boy Patti planned on dancing with.

In the whirl of frenzied preparations and general excitement, Patti felt less uneasy about deceiving her father. Lucky for her, her father was too busy with his own plans for the evening to worry about hers. Gus Hamilton, an old friend of his, had arranged for him to go out on a blind date—his first since his wife had died. They were going to dinner and a play in Sacramento, and Gus, his wife, and a woman named Charity Wilcox would be picking him up. Patti had never seen her dad so nervous. She could have almost believed he was fifteen instead of fifty.

As if on cue, Frank Curtis stuck his head through the doorway. "Katie—I can't find my blue-striped tie!" His broad face was flushed with panic, and Patti noticed several bits of Kleenex were sticking to his chin where he'd cut himself shaving.

"Such an emergency!" cried Katie, throwing up her arms. "Between the two of you, I need four hands."

Mr. Curtis caught sight of his daughter and whistled. "Hey, don't you look sensational. If I didn't know better, I'd swear somebody traded my daughter in for Brooke Shields."

Patti blushed. "Oh, Daddy—" She located a

bare spot on his cheek and gave him a quick, embarrassed peck. "You look pretty outrageous yourself."

"I'm assuming that's a compliment?"

She giggled. "Of course, Dad."

They were interrupted by the chiming of the doorbell.

Patti's father groaned. "Good old Ham. Never late for an appointment. You're sure I look all right? You don't think I should have worn my brown suit instead?" He darted a last, nervous look at the mirror.

"Relax, Dad, you look fine. You don't want to look too good in case she's a three-hundred-pound elephant or something."

But Charity Wilcox wasn't a three-hundred-pound elephant. What she was, Patti saw when she entered the living room behind her father, was a very shapely, attractive if not overly affected lady—fortyish, with sprayed platinum hair that was done up in a lot of little swirls, and long, long false eyelashes that started fluttering as if a motor had been turned on the minute she laid eyes on Frank Curtis.

"Oooh, I'm sooo pleased to meet you," she cried, extending a beautifully manicured hand as she moved slowly forward. "Ham's told me sooo much about you." Flutter, flutter. "But he didn't tell me how handsome you are, the devil!" Ham raised his shoulders to protest, but his wife stopped him.

Patti's father flushed, looking pleased and embarrassed. Patti wanted to throw up. He shook Charity's hand, mumbling something about how happy he was to meet her, too. He didn't have to say that he thought she was a knockout—the grin plastered across his face was better than a thousand words.

"And *this* must be your little girl!" In a cloud of fruity perfume, Charity descended on Patti, who took a quick step backward when it looked as if she were in danger of having her cheeks pinched. "Isn't she just sooo precious."

"Patti's on her way to a dance at school," Mr. Curtis announced.

Charity seized upon that. "How lovely! Your very first dance," she said cooing, as if Patti were all of twelve years old. "Oh, I wish I could turn the clock back and be young and pretty again," she added wistfully.

This, of course, had the intended effect of eliciting compliments from both men that she was still ravishing and looked twenty years younger than her age. *Baloney!* Patti thought. She was glad to see that Mrs. Hamilton, a sensible, sophisticated, and attractively gray-haired woman, looked disgusted, too.

Her father's reaction was another story. He couldn't take his eyes off Charity Wilcox. He wore a silly grin that got bigger and bigger each time she fluttered her lashes at him or rested one of her hands on his sleeve. Patti couldn't believe it. Her father, who considered himself such a great judge of character!

In disbelief she watched them trail out the front door with Charity hanging on her father's arm. Ugh! How could her dad, who thought Tim was a troublemaker, not see that Charity Wilcox was *really* trouble?

The more she thought about it, the more unfair it seemed.

Chapter Nine

The dance was in full swing by the time Patti and Tracy arrived. They stepped into an auditorium transformed by colored lights, thin strips of green crepe paper, leis, and cardboard scenes of the tropics—including a blazing sunset and a secluded bridge. Loud band music spilled from a stage festooned with paper palm trees and tropical fruits.

"Don't you just love it?" cried Tracy over the noise. She'd been on the dance committee and had talked of little else for the past week. "You wouldn't believe how long it took just to get the cardboard scenery set up, with all the bananas and pineapples we had to cut out. It took nearly a week."

Suddenly Patti spotted Tim through the crowd, and her pulse leaped. He was walking toward her, and he looked absolutely gorgeous in dark slacks, tawny sport coat, and light yellow shirt, all of which set off his deep tan. As his blue eyes swept over her appreciatively, Tim flashed her his most captivating grin.

"If I didn't know you, Patti Curtis, I'd swear you were one of those goddesses out of Greek mythology—what was her name? Oh yeah, Aphrodite, the goddess of love."

"Flattery will get you everywhere." She laughed and slipped easily into his arms.

"Just as long as it gets us onto the dance floor." His gaze took in Tracy. "Hey, Trace. You look super, too. Is that real?" He pointed to the red rose pinned over her ear.

"Silk," she said. "That way it doesn't wilt even when I do—as they say in the hair spray commercials." Then she was gone, as a tall, red-haired boy took her arm, and the two were absorbed into the pulsing crowd.

Tim led Patti over to a relatively uncrowded spot, his arms tightening around her as they began moving to the slow, easy beat of a Barbra Streisand song. He was just tall enough so that their bodies meshed perfectly. His jacket tickled her bare arms, and as she pressed her head against his shoulder, she caught the light scent of soap and aftershave. Happiness welled up inside her, so sharply sweet it brought a mist of tears to her eyes.

Tim's mouth traced her cheek lightly, finding her lips in a long, deep kiss that turned her knees to putty. "Do you know how special you are to me?" he murmured.

Patti's throat was so tight she couldn't find the words to express what she was feeling.. *I love you, Tim,* her heart cried out. It was the first time she had let herself think those words, having been afraid of growing too involved before she had time to sort out all her confusing emotions. Now there was no going back. She had fallen in love with Tim—and there was nothing anybody could do, including her father, to change it.

She snuggled against him, wanting that wonderful, magical moment to last forever.

The rest of the dance was a blur of whirling shapes and the throbbing of electric guitars. Slow songs blended into fast, and back again. Tim never once let her out of his sight; when they weren't dancing, she could feel the firm pressure of his hand in the small of her back, guiding her across the crowded floor toward the refreshment tables or the rows of folding chairs lining the walls. In the shadows they kissed, his lips nuzzling her ear, or his fingers playing with a stray lock of her hair. A single thought played over and over in Patti's mind against the backdrop of noise and shuffling feet: *We belong together, no matter what anyone says.*

On the dance floor Patti caught sight of Jamie and Denise locked in a tight embrace and gazing rapturously into each other's eyes even though the song was a fast one. Patti attempted several times to get her friend's attention, but finally she gave up when she saw that Denise had eyes for no one but Jamie.

They sailed past Gayle and Sandy, who dipped and spun to the beat as if they were riding skateboards down a winding slope. Gayle gestured frantically over Sandy's head at a couple dancing near the fire exit. Patti craned her neck in response, spotting two of the chaperones swaying in each other's arms—Ms. Ketchum and Mr. Reese.

"If this was a Disney movie, I could see them as Miss Skunk and Mr. Ostrich," said Patti, giggling. "I can't imagine a more unlikely couple."

"You never know about some people," Tim replied.

Patti, thinking briefly of her father and Charity, silently agreed.

The highlight of the evening was when Laura Appleby, who thought of herself as Deborah Harry the Second, got up to sing and one of the guitarists accidentally spilled punch down the front of her skintight lemon-colored jumpsuit. You could hear her amplified shrieks all the way out to the parking lot, as it was later claimed by Elaine Baumgarten, who had been necking in the car with her boyfriend Jimmy at the time. The photographer for the school paper even caught a great candid shot of Laura beating the guitarist over the head with the empty paper cup.

The same photographer was also on hand to take pictures of couples in front of the tropical sunset scene. Patti felt her first small stab of unhappiness as she watched the kids she knew drifting over to wait in line. They would have something from this night they would always treasure, while she and Tim . . .

It was just too risky for them to have their picture taken together. Her dad might see it, and he would know she had deceived him. Trying to untangle her thoughts and emotions, Patti suddenly felt on the verge of tears. How, she wondered, could doing something your parents considered wrong *feel* so right at the same time?

Tim sensed her shift of mood and suggested they take a walk outside. Hand in hand they strolled down to the empty quad, where they sat and talked until the distant flutter of music from the auditorium finally drifted off into silence. A couple Patti recognized as Bill Zeigler and Martha Beal materialized from the shadows and waved gaily in their direction.

"Hey, you two, a bunch of us are going into town for a pizza," Bill called. "You wanna come?"

"Thanks," Tim yelled. "Some other time!"

The clear night was heavy with stars, and a warm breeze played with the silken folds of Patti's dress as Tim drew her to her feet and kissed her gently.

"We'd better get back," he whispered huskily. "Tracy'll be looking for you."

"Oh, Tim, I wish—"

He silenced her with another, deeper kiss. "I know. I wish it, too. You know, I really am starting to feel like we're some kind of damn Romeo and Juliet."

"We've got to do something," Patti said fiercely.

"What?"

"We've got to think of a way to get our parents together and talk this thing out. We can't go on like this forever—sneaking around like—like we're criminals or something."

"You're right," Tim agreed grimly. "We've got to take action sooner or later—it might as well be sooner. Only it could backfire on us, you know. Putting our parents together in one room could end up making Pearl Harbor look like a spitball fight."

Patti sighed. "I guess that's a chance we'll just have to take."

Chapter Ten

"I don't know, Pattycake—" Frank Curtis stopped buttering his toast and looked up at his daughter. "I invited Charity to have dinner with us tomorrow night, nothing fancy, but I thought we—"

Patti nearly choked on the piece of bacon she was chewing. "But it'd only be for an hour or so. Just a little get-together so the parents of the choir members can meet each other. I'm sure Charity, uh, would enjoy meeting everybody. She seems, um—the—uh—friendly type."

"Well—"

"Please, Dad, I promise they won't stay long. This is important—the final rehearsal is in two days."

And it *was* important, but not for that reason. It was all part of the plan she and Tim had worked out for getting her father

109

and his mother together in a neutral situation. Actually, it was mostly Patti's idea, and she thought it was a pretty brilliant one at that. Her father still didn't know that Tim was in the choir with her—she'd been evasive on the subject—and neither did Tim's busy mother. So it was a fairly simple matter to get them together under one roof without their knowing about it beforehand. As for what would happen after that—well, she'd have to worry about that when the time came. Both she and Tim were willing to bet their parents were too civilized to scream at each other in front of everyone else.

But Mr. Curtis was still hedging. "Well, I—"

"*Please*, Daddy, I'm sure Charity would just *love* it!" Her own insincerity made her want to throw up.

But it was convincing enough as far as her father was concerned. "I suppose it wouldn't hurt. Charity's coming over at eight—"

"Super! I'll tell everyone to come by seven-thirty. And don't worry about the refreshments—the kids are pitching in."

"Anybody I know?" he asked, crunching down on a neat triangle of toast.

"Uh, I don't think so." Patti pretended a sudden interest in picking the chocolate sprinkles from a doughnut.

Her father peered curiously at her. "What in heaven's name are you doing?" he asked, as the pile of sprinkles on her plate grew larger.

"I can't eat them," she explained, grimacing. "They remind me of ants."

He sighed, burying himself under the morning paper. "Honestly, Patti, I don't think I'll ever understand you."

That makes two of us, she added silently.

Gayle and her father were the first to arrive Wednesday night—Gayle's mother had the flu and couldn't come. But Gayle knew all about the plan and wanted to be there early "to get in on the action," as she put it. Patti smiled as the image of her dad and Tim's mom wearing boxing gloves popped into her mind.

She saw her father's eyes bug out and his smile widen when he was introduced to Mr. Summers. Gayle's father was wearing skintight pants and a clingy flowered shirt, open at the neck to display a Fort Knox of gold chains and medallions—making him look as if he would be more at home in Las Vegas than in Clinton. Patti was used to him by now, but she still thought it would be strange to have a father right out of *Saturday Night Fever.*

"Nice place. I see you're into Early American," he commented, surveying the living room through blue-tinted lenses.

Not everyone in the choir was able to come, but by ten minutes to eight Patti had counted at least thirty people, including Mr. Reese, Martha Beal and her parents, and Gabe North, who'd brought along his grandmother, a spry, silver-haired woman in a gold lamé pantsuit, who told stories about when she was a Rockette with the Radio City Music Hall. Patti was having such a good time, she forgot to watch the clock. But when eight-fifteen rolled around and Tim still hadn't arrived, she began to grow nervous.

Then Charity Wilcox arrived in a whirlwind of pink frills and suffocating perfume, and Patti, in her disgust, forgot everything else. Gayle and Martha agreed that Charity was something else.

"Why is it when I look at her, I get this sudden craving for cotton candy?" whispered Gayle.

"She looks like our Avon lady," muttered Martha as she took a bite of liverwurst and Ry-Krisp. "Actually, our ex-Avon lady—she ran off with her neighbor's husband. Underneath all that pink frosting, they're the worst kind. Barracudas."

"Thanks for the warning," Patti said grimly as Charity proceeded to drape herself over her father's arm, taking coy little sips of his wine even though she had her own glass.

Suddenly Charity caught her eye and darted over. "I'm soooo glad you wanted me to meet your friends, Patti honey." She oozed familiarity. "Makes me almost feel like one of the family. Now I want to hear all about this little concert you're singing in. I hear you're gonna be on TV—"

Fortunately Patti was rescued at that moment by the chiming of the doorbell. It was Tim and his mother. Patti was so glad to see him she nearly threw her arms around him on the spot, but Tim shot her a warning look.

"Patti, I'd like you to meet my mother," he said.

Ann McBride wasn't what Patti had expected at all. She was very tiny, with curly blond hair—natural—and the same blue, blue eyes as Tim. She wore no makeup except a touch of lipstick and mascara, and her only jewelry was a thin gold chain to accent her herringbone pantsuit. With her pert, healthy looks and lightly freckled nose, Ann McBride looked more like a cheerleader than somebody's mother, Patti decided.

Before she could open her mouth to say anything, Frank Curtis spotted them and rushed over. "What are *you* doing here?" he demanded.

Tim's mother looked just as startled, but she quickly regained her composure and smiled sweetly. "I would have asked you the same question, except it appears I'm in the wrong house. Obviously," she added, her steely gaze resting on Tim, "there's been a mistake."

Mr. Curtis fixed Patti with an equally menacing glare. "Young lady, do you mind telling me what this is all about?"

Patti tried her best to look innocent. "I don't know what you mean, Dad. Tim's in the choir, and—"

"And you two figured you could trick us into getting together, am I right?" he interrupted sternly.

To her credit, Ann looked almost amused by the whole thing. "I don't suppose you can really blame them, Frank. After all, this whole thing *has* gotten out of hand. Since I'm here, why don't you stop being such a fuddy-duddy and get me a drink. I could use one right now."

Patti's father turned red but didn't argue as he stalked off. A few minutes later, Patti, Tim, and Ann, drink in hand, followed him into the kitchen where they could talk in privacy.

"Now let's get one thing straight here," he began. "I'm not unreasonable, but a man can only be pushed so far—"

"I think the same can be said for a woman," interrupted Ann, lifting one eyebrow.

Patti and Tim exchanged looks. So far, not so good.

"You know, Mom, I've been thinking," Tim put in. "It might make things easier if I agree to split the damages on the car with Mr. Curtis's company."

"We're talking about what's fair, Tim, not what's easy," she said.

"In that case—" Frank Curtis started to say.

"I should pay for everything, since the whole thing was my fault," Patti supplied eagerly. "Look, Dad, if you don't agree with me, I'll pay for it myself as soon as I get the money."

"Whose idea was *that*?" her father asked, staring pointedly at Tim.

Ann McBride drew herself up to her full five feet as if she were the Statue of Liberty. "Now just a minute, Frank Curtis, my son isn't in the habit of trying to swindle innocent people out of their money. As a matter of fact, I have no interest in your daughter's money. Your company has an obligation, and I'm going to see that you fulfill it!"

"We'll certainly see about that!"

"Dad—" Patti pleaded, knowing it was no use.

"Forget it, Patti," Tim said in a tight voice. "We should've known he wouldn't listen."

Instantly she bristled. Somehow the very thoughts she had been thinking sounded different coming from Tim. Anger about everything that had happened that night boiled up in her.

"What about *her*?" she demanded, pointing at Tim's mother.

Tim's face flushed a dark red. "Well, it's pretty obvious, isn't it? Any father who refuses to let his daughter go out with a boy he's never even met—"

Patti was dangerously close to crying. "Who— who says I want to go out with you anyway, Tim McBride?"

"If that's the way you feel about it—that's just fine with me!" He glared at her, blue eyes flashing.

Leaping from her chair, Patti left Ann and her father to stare at each other in amazement as she whirled from the kitchen—only to collide head-on with Charity Wilcox in the hallway.

Charity scarcely noticed her, though. Patti saw, through a veil of tears, that she was too busy purring and fluttering her eyelashes at Mr. Summers to pay attention to anything else—even Frank Curtis, who stood glowering in the doorway. And the worst part of it was, Patti got absolutely no satisfaction from it.

Chapter Eleven

"Talk about World War Three!" Patti said and moaned. "It was awful, just awful, Denise. My dad and Tim's mom were yelling at each other, then I started in on Tim. Oohhh—every time I think about it I feel sick!"

They were climbing the stairs to Ms. Ketchum's class, and Denise paused to peer closely at her friend. "I thought you looked kind of pale. Are you really sick?"

Patty nodded miserably. She had woken up that morning with sniffles and a scratchy throat, which she figured had been brought on by all the crying she'd done the night before. Also, she had probably only slept a total of two hours. Long after everyone had gone home—including Charity, who had stomped off in a huff after Patti's father told her what he thought of her—she had lain awake listening for the phone, half-hoping

Tim would call to apologize and half-wanting to call him and apologize herself. But neither of them made the first move, and by morning Patti felt exhausted as she dragged herself out of bed to go to school.

"But I can't be really sick!" she cried in desperation. "The final rehearsal is tonight. Mr. Reese is counting on me."

Denise gave her a sly wink. "Don't worry. I think I know a cure for what's wrong with you. Have you tried talking to Tim?"

"Forget it. He doesn't want to see me."

"How do you know that?"

"He told me so last night. Anyway, if he'd wanted to apologize, he would've called last night, wouldn't he?"

"Who said anything about apologizing? I said 'talk.' Have you ever heard of compromise? You know, like, 'I was wrong, and you were wrong, so let's forget the whole thing?' "

"In that case, why doesn't he compromise with me?"

"Boy, Curtis, you can be so dense sometimes! If it was Jamie and me, I'd be over there so fast you wouldn't see my feet touch the ground."

Patti was unsure. "Well—I don't know."

Denise paused at the top of the stairwell to

give her a long, hard look. "You know who you're starting to remind me of?"

Patti sighed. "Who am I starting to remind you of?"

"Your father!"

Patti started to say something, but the bell rang, and they raced down the hall to the classroom and slid into their seats. As luck would have it, Ms. Ketchum had chosen that day, of all days, to spring a pop quiz. Patti stared unseeingly at the sheet of questions until one in particular swam up at her. It was about the difference between a simile and a metaphor, and she had to give a related example of each.

Without having to think, Patti wrote:

Simile: She was as stubborn as a mule.
Metaphor: She was a stubborn mule.

After giving a lot of thought to what Denise had said, Patti decided to track Tim down at lunchtime. It was silly, she realized, to worry about who apologized to whom first. But he wasn't in any of the places he usually hung out, so she finally gave up looking. The a cappella choir met last period, but Tim was not in class. Patti began to feel sicker. Her throat was still sore, and she had trouble reaching some of the high notes, which prompted a concerned Mr. Reese to prescribe liberal doses of honey and lemon.

After the last bell rang, Patti rushed over to Tim's locker to wait for him there. She knew she wouldn't even have to say she was sorry—he would know in an instant just by looking at her face. She imagined his muscular arms encircling her, his lips telling her without words that everything was all right between them. . . .

That was when she spotted him rounding the corner—so deep in conversation with Honey Jenkins he didn't even notice her. Blond, blue-eyed, gorgeous Honey Jenkins, the high-school equivalent of Charity Wilcox. Patti's heart sank. Everyone at McKinley knew that Tim and Honey had gone together the year before. Tim swore there was nothing between them now, but . . .

The way he was looking at her turned Patti's stomach. Honey was wearing skintight designer jeans with a chic maroon pullover that clung to her ample curves. While she looked as if she wasn't trying at all to be sexy, anyone could tell she most certainly was making the effort. Tim bent his head close, and whatever he said must have struck her as hilarious, because all of a sudden she was all over him, holding on to his arm and leaning up against him as if she couldn't walk on her own. And Tim didn't seem to mind one bit. In fact, Patti was devastated to observe, he looked as if he were enjoying himself immensely.

Patti bolted down the corridor before he could catch sight of her. Tears ran down her cheeks, and she felt as if she would never again be able to draw a normal breath. By the time she reached home, she ached all over, her throat was burning, and she had a temperature of a hundred and one—not to mention a broken heart.

The final rehearsal was at seven, and Patti was determined not to miss it—even if she was on her deathbed, which it certainly did feel like. A few minutes before Gayle was supposed to pick her up, she washed her face with cold water, took four aspirins, and a fistful of vitamin C tablets, and jammed a box of cough drops into her purse. She was pulling on her heaviest Shetland sweater when Gayle's VW beeped for her out in the driveway.

"Good luck, Pattycake," Mr. Curtis called from his easy chair as she headed out the door. Patti noticed that he seemed subdued, but she was too miserable herself to give it much consideration. "In case I haven't gotten around to telling you lately, I want you to know I'm really proud of you. I can't wait to see you up on that stage tomorrow night."

"Thanks, Dad," she muttered, fleeing outside before he had a chance to notice or comment on how terrible she looked. She had been hiding out in her room since she got home from school, so they hadn't talked all evening. Or maybe he was just being tactful, she thought.

Tact was the last thing on Gayle's mind as Patti dropped into the bucket seat beside her. "Hey, you look awful," she said. "What happened?"

Patti glared at her. "Thanks, Gayle. You really know how to calm a person's butterflies."

Gayle was instantly apologetic. "Hey, don't listen to me, what do I know? I just thought—" She started out in second gear, and the car gave a little lurch "Well, Denise told me about you and Tim. Gee, Patti, what a crummy thing to happen. Do you think you'll make up?"

Denise and her big mouth, thought Patti. "Not if Honey Jenkins has her way," she muttered.

"Huh?" yelled Gayle over the loud noise of the ancient engine.

"I said," Patti cleared her throat, "would you like a honey cough drop?" She held out the box.

"Thanks," said Gayle, giving her a funny look as she popped one in her mouth. "But if you ask me, cough drops aren't going to solve your problems."

At school Patti slipped into her choir robe and applied fresh lipstick. The next evening, for television, she would have to wear a lot more makeup. "To keep us all from looking like ghosts," explained Martha. She peered closely at Patti. "Speaking of ghosts, you look pretty pale yourself, Patti. Are you OK?"

Patti was saved from having to answer when Mr. Reese stuck his head through the doorway. "Five minutes, people."

"Where are my glasses?" wailed Sylvia Bridges. "How can I read the music without my glasses?"

"Try looking on your nose!" Melanie Harper called out impatiently.

Patti's stomach balled into a tight fist of panic. How could she sing the way she felt right now? She was not only sick, but miserable. The image of Tim and Honey played over and over inside her head like a scratched record. She was afraid that when she looked at him, she would get so choked up she wouldn't be able to squeeze out a single note. How could loving someone the way she loved Tim be so wonderful one minute, and so awful the next?

Just as Patti feared, nothing seemed to go right from the very beginning. She was fine when everyone else was singing, but when she had to sing the soprano part in a quartet, she was so nervous her voice cracked several times. Mr. Reese frowned, and she thought she would die of humiliation.

They sang the "Pilgrims' Chorus" from Wagner's *Tannhäuser*, followed by a madrigal and a gospel number. Then came *Elijah*, in which both Patti and Tim had solos. Listening to his rich tenor soar out over the auditorium, she was sure her heart would break, and when it was her turn, her throat was so tight with unshed tears, it caused her voice to emerge as a whisper in comparison to Tim's. She had to strain to reach the high notes, several of which wobbled out of control— evoking another grimace from Mr. Reese.

"Patti, Patti, Patti!" he said, taking her aside during the brief intermission. "You're not projecting! I can barely hear you! Think of all those people in the back rows tomorrow night."

"I—I'll try, Mr. Reese." She gulped, sensing it was no use.

The harder she tried to unfreeze herself, the worse it seemed to get. By the end of the concert, she was so embarrassed she wished a trapdoor would open up at her feet so she could drop out of sight. She was blinking back tears as she climbed down off the bleachers. Her only thought was to escape as quickly as possible.

"Patti, I want to talk to you," Mr. Reese called after her as she blindly made her way toward the fire exit.

She knew what he was going to say, but she knew also that if she had to hear it she wouldn't be able to control her tears any longer. She had ruined it—for everyone. Mr. Reese would tell her not to bother showing up for tomorrow night's performance. And, of course, he was right. She knew he was right, but that didn't make it any easier. Misery throbbed in her chest.

Tim's voice broke through the roaring in her ears. "Patti, wait—"

But she couldn't stop herself from running away. As the door banged shut behind her, she charged out into the darkness of the quad, the cool night air slapping her burning cheeks. She didn't even stop long enough to pull on her jeans or slip out of her robe or figure out which direction she was running in. She just knew she had to get as far away as possible.

Chapter Twelve

It was three miles from school to Patti's house—a breeze on her ten-speed, but on foot in the darkness, it seemed an impossibly long distance. Especially, Patti thought, when you were dumb enough to take a "short cut," only to get hopelessly lost.

There was a vast field stretching beyond the school grounds that had once been grazing land. Now it was just acres and acres of weeds, with a creek running through it and a narrow path cutting across one corner where kids had beaten down a path on the way to school. Patti herself had often taken the path, which cut across to the highway, but never before at night. Somewhere in the moonless blackness, she had taken a wrong turn, and now, as she stumbled along knee-deep in grass, not being able to see in any direction, Patti realized that she hadn't the vaguest idea where she was going. She had long ago left the lights of the school behind, and as she listened for the sounds of cars that would lead her to the highway, all she could hear was the frantic chirping of crickets over the soft sigh of the wind rippling the grass.

Why had she been so stupid as to run out like that? Instead of facing up to the mess she had created back there, she had only succeeded in making it worse! Not only would Tim hate her, but he'd think she was a hopeless idiot as well. Everyone would. After this, she would never be able to show her face at school.

"Help!" she yelped, a feeble cry that did little good except to pierce the dense, frightening silence surrounding her.

Of course, she told herself, she could always wait until morning to find her way home. But by then she would probably be dead from exposure or from stepping on a rattlesnake. The fact that it was a warm night and that there were no rattlesnakes in the area, didn't stop her from feeling sorry for herself.

She wasn't wearing her watch, but she guessed she'd been wandering around for more than an hour. Her legs were damp and itchy where the muddy hem of her robe dragged on her ankles, and her progress had slowed to a crawl. *Why didn't I at least bother to change?* she berated herself. *If anyone saw me now, they'd think I was the Creature from the Black Lagoon.* The thought almost made her laugh, but she hiccuped softly instead.

They would have phoned her father. No doubt he was worried sick and combing the town in search of her. Patti wondered how she could have been so deceitful to him; all he had ever tried to do was protect her, and she had ended up hating him for it. True, he sometimes went overboard on strictness, but she knew it was only because he loved her. It wasn't as if he was doing it to be mean. She thought of all the times her own selfishness must have hurt him. Why was it, she asked herself, that it always took something really terrible to happen before one could see things in a clear light?

She felt bad about the way she had acted toward Tim, too. Denise was right—she hadn't even given him a chance, either to apologize or explain. She had let her stubborn pride get in the way, then had immediately jumped to conclusions about Honey Jenkins without even giving Tim the benefit of the doubt. Would he have been so quick to doubt her?

Didn't loving someone mean trusting them, too?

It was like a bad dream—Tim—the final rehearsal—her being lost. If it wasn't actually happening, she never would have believed it. Patti shivered, feeling dizzy because of tiredness and the slight fever she was running. She stopped to slap at a mosquito that had landed on her arm.

That was when she heard it—a distant drone of a car. She was close to the highway after all! A sudden surge of energy pushed her forward even as the sound of the engine died away. She couldn't see where she was going, but that didn't stop her from breaking into a run. Clutching the heavy skirt of her robe about her, she ran toward a pinpoint of light that appeared on the horizon. At first she thought it was a firefly, then, as she got closer, she saw it was the bobbing beam of a flashlight.

"Hey, I'm over here!" she shouted at the faceless dark figure in the distance.

In the darkness Patti didn't see the tangle of rusted barbed wire at her feet. It snagged on her robe, and the last thing she remembered was the ground being snatched out from under her and something hard smacking her on the forehead.

*   *   *

"Patti . . . you're all right, Patti. You just got the wind knocked out of you."

Through the buzzing in her ears, Patti became aware of a faint voice, then a pair of strong male arms lifting her up, carrying her somewhere. She felt safe and protected, like waking from a nightmare and finding herself snuggled safely in bed. Her eyes fluttered open. Groggily she blinked up at the face that hovered over hers.

"Tim? . . . Tim! How did you find me?"

He grinned. "You can thank your own lungs for that. I would have heard you halfway to Sacramento."

"Ouch!" she fingered the lump that was beginning to form over her left eye. Tim set her down gently in the front seat of his car.

"Clumsy as ever," he said jokingly, though she detected a note of trembling relief underneath. "Don't worry, I think you'll live. I'm not so sure about me, though. I hope you realize that was one helluva scare you gave me."

"Oh, Tim—I'm so sorry!"

"When I couldn't find you at school, I called your dad. We looked everywhere before I thought of this field. He even thought you might have been kidnapped! He's phoning the sheriff's office right now."

Huddled in the blanket Tim had tucked around her, Patti felt very small and ashamed. "I'm sorry," she repeated. "I guess I wasn't thinking straight when I ran out back there. All I could think of was how bad I blew it."

"You thought that because of a few crummy mistakes?" Tim bellowed at her angrily. "Boy, do you have something coming on that score! *Everyone* has a bad performance now and then—it's nothing to freak out about. You should've been glad it wasn't the real thing, that's all."

Patti offered him a weak smile. "You sure have a way of putting things in perspective. I bet you think I'm pretty dumb."

He relaxed. "Dumb, but cute."

"You don't hate me?"

"Why should I hate you? We had a little argument the other night—who said it all has to be hearts and flowers?"

She drew a long, shaky breath. "But when I saw you with Honey Jenkins—"

"Honey! What's she got to do with this?"

Voicing her fears aloud made Patti feel even more ridiculous. "I saw you walking with her after school, and I guess I thought . . . I—I thought you and she . . ." she let the sentence trail into silence.

She expected Tim to grow angry again, but instead he only laughed. Reaching across the driver's seat, he gathered her in his arms, holding her tightly until she began to feel his warmth seeping into her.

"You know something?" he murmured huskily. "I must be crazy to fall in love with someone who not only bashes my car but is so thickheaded she doesn't even know how much I care about her."

Patti snuggled deeper into his embrace and sighed contentedly. "Tim? About the other night, I wanted you to know how sorry I was for the way I acted."

"Hey, me, too. We both got kind of carried away, didn't we?"

"About my dad—"

He silenced her with a deep, melting kiss. "Don't worry. I have a feeling that that one'll work itself out. Right now, I've got to get you home. Your dad's been out of his mind worrying about you." He drew back and looked at her, as if seeing her for the first time. "Man, he's never gonna believe you weren't trampled by a herd of elephants!"

Patti laughed. "I'm afraid to even imagine what I must look like."

Tim grinned at her as he started the engine. "Right now, on a scale of one to ten, I'd say about minus twelve. So that must prove it."

"Prove what?" she asked.

"That love is blind."

Chapter Thirteen

Patti's father hugged her so tightly she could scarcely breathe.

"Thank God you're all right! I should probably give you the dickens for scaring me half to death, but I'm so glad to see you're all right. You are, aren't you? It's a little hard to tell—you look like you've been dragged a mile behind a horse."

Patti grimaced. "Believe it or not, Dad, I feel great."

"Well, a hot bath won't hurt. I know I'll feel a lot better seeing you cleaned up and tucked in bed."

"Oh, Dad," Patti said, shaking her head, but she was smiling as she said it.

Mr. Curtis turned to Tim, standing quietly out of the way, and offered him his hand. "What with all the confusion, I never did get a chance to thank you, young man. I owe you a lot."

Tim shrugged, looking slightly uncomfortable under this new friendly scrutiny. "Patti wasn't in any danger, Mr. Curtis. Anyway, it was just a lucky guess about the field."

"I'd call it levelheaded thinking," he corrected, "and that's a lot more than I've been doing lately. I'm afraid I owe you an apology, too. I was letting my pigheadedness stand in the way of fair judgment."

Tim ducked his head and smiled sheepishly. "Hey, forget it, Mr. Curtis. Remember, you weren't the only one."

Patti seconded the motion with a hearty sneeze.

Her father turned to her and glared at her. "Why are you standing there grinning like the Cheshire cat? I'm not so stuck in my ways I don't know when I'm wrong. And if it hadn't been for your tricks and arguments, I probably would have seen it a lot sooner, too!" As Patti sputtered in protest, he added, "Now, scoot. Get off to bed before I remember you're too old for a spanking. Don't worry about us, Tim and I have some getting acquainted to do."

When she finally left them, her father was

heating up milk for hot cocoa, and the two were chatting like old friends.

"I know I don't look like it now," Mr. Curtis was saying, "but when I was your age, I was fullback for our team."

"No kidding, Mr. Curtis? Hey, I'll bet you were pretty good."

"Ninety-eight point six!" pronounced Katie with a triumphant flourish of the thermometer. "You see what a good night's sleep and a cup of my sassafras tea can do? Now open wide, and let me have a look at that throat."

As Patti obeyed, Katie bent over the bed, peering intently into her open mouth. "Mmmm. Still a bit red. But don't worry, we'll have it fixed in no time. I know just the thing. By tonight, the star soprano soloist will be as good as new."

Patti sighed, snuggling back down under the covers. She'd been so happy the night before after making up with Tim that she hadn't given a thought to what it would be like facing Mr. Reese again. In spite of Tim's reassurances, she still dreaded the outcome of the disastrous rehearsal. What if he decided to let someone else replace her? Well, she honestly couldn't blame him if he did.

Her father had called the school to let Mr.

Reese know what had happened and to tell him she'd be staying home to rest up for the night's performance. Patti expected the phone to ring at any moment; she was sure that as soon as Mr. Reese got the message, he'd call back to tell her not to bother getting out of bed at all. And even if he didn't, she still wasn't sure she'd have the courage to get back up on the stage after what had happened.

"What's this I see?" asked Katie. "Cold feet, already?"

Patti wiggled her toes under the blanket. "My feet are fine—it's my nerves I'm worried about. How do I know I won't blow it again like last night?"

"You don't," replied Katie, giving a brisk, no-nonsense shake of her head. "And you never will unless you try."

The phone rang, and Patti jumped. Katie went to answer it. "For you, Patti!" she called from down the hall.

It was Mr. Reese.

"Patti!" his voice boomed at her as if he were standing right beside her. She winced. "You had us pretty worried last night. You sure you're OK?"

"I—I'm fine, Mr. Reese," she stammered, waiting for the ax to fall.

"Patti, I think you should know—"

She held her breath.

"—that what happened at the final rehearsal could have happened to anyone. I was going to tell you that last night, but you ran out so fast I never got the chance."

Patti let her breath out with a whoosh. "That's what Tim said."

"Well, he's right, you know." He chuckled. "I'll let you in on a secret I've never told any of my students before. A few years back when I was in an opera company, I had my big chance at singing the part of Rigoletto. And what do you suppose happened on opening night? Just as I was launching into my aria—my mind went totally blank! Well, I can tell you my face was red—to say the least. But as you can see, I survived. Except for a few scratches to my ego."

Patti breathed a deep sigh. "Thanks Mr. Reese. I guess I don't feel so bad anymore."

He became his gruff self once again. "Remember, I'm expecting you to be dynamite tonight. Can I count on you?"

"You bet!"

Tim stopped by after school to see Patti, then he and Mr. Curtis spent an hour in the den going over the estimates Tim had gotten to repair his car. After talking it over the previous night, Tim had agreed that he had been partially to blame for the accident—if only in a minor way. Mr. Curtis pointed out that there was a thing known as "contributory negligence," such as not looking carefully enough when backing out of a parking space. Tim also admitted that it had been pretty reckless of him to be driving without insurance, which Patti's father didn't argue with. Instead, he promised to see if he could get Tim more reasonable rates than those he was paying. Meanwhile, he would arrange for the damages to be paid, minus the hundred dollars Tim agreed was a fair amount to deduct as his share.

"Now, the only problem I can see," Mr. Curtis said, "is getting your mother to agree to this arrangement and call off the dogs."

Tim laughed. "I don't know. She can be pretty prickly."

"Yeah, I know. Kind of reminds me of myself."

"Tell her," Patti interjected, "that if my dad can change his mind, *anyone* can."

"You're right," Tim said, "but I hate to be the one to tell her."

"In this case," said Mr. Curtis, his sober expression unable to disguise the twinkle in his eye, "I'd have to recommend a little old-fashioned diplomacy." When Patti and Tim exchanged doubtful looks, he added mischievously, "I think you two would call it trickery."

"Dad, you wouldn't!"

"Seems to me you weren't above using a little of the same on Ann and me once before," he observed archly.

"What did you have in mind?" asked Tim.

"Well, now," he said, leaning back in his chair, "I have an idea, but I'm going to keep it to myself and surprise you. After all, you never know when a plan might backfire."

"Good luck," Tim said. "I just hope I'm not around if it does backfire."

Mr. Curtis put his arm around Patti's shoulders and gave her a little squeeze. "Looks like both of us are going to need all the luck we can get, right, Pattycake?"

Chapter Fourteen

"Nervous?" Tim asked.

They were standing backstage with a few minutes left before they would have to take their places on the bleachers.

"A little," Patti confessed, though, surprisingly enough, her butterflies were almost under control.

He squeezed her hand reassuringly and grinned. "Well, anyway, you *look* sensational."

"Thanks to Katie's wizardry." Not only had she cured Patti's sore throat with her herbal concoctions, but she'd come to the rescue with needle and thread to repair her robe, and she had applied a little makeup to Patti's bruise. "You look pretty dashing yourself."

"Yeah," Tim chuckled, "I've always thought I looked good in skirts."

Gayle spotted them and rushed over. "My gosh, how can you be laughing at a time like this? I'm so nervous I could die! I've never been on TV before!"

"Relax, Gayle," Patti said. "Remember all those pep talks you gave me? You've got to think positive. And remember—if I can, anyone can."

"Anything! As long as I don't have to think about all those people out there. My parents are sitting in the front row. Do you believe it? Out of the whole auditorium they had to go and choose the front row!"

Tim gave Patti a meaningful look. "Speaking of parents. I haven't seen my mom anywhere. Has your father shown up yet?"

Patti peeked through the curtain. There was Denise and her whole family—occupying most of the third row. She caught sight of Ms. Ketchum and Mrs. Jaffe. A lot of faces she recognized from school, but there were just as many unfamiliar ones. Suddenly she saw something that caused her to clutch frantically at Tim's sleeve.

"Look! Over there in the back. Isn't that—?"

"Mom!" cried Tim.

"Sitting with *my father!*"

They stared at each other in disbelief.

"I wonder how—" Tim started to say, but Mr. Reese motioned for them to take their places.

The concert—in spite of everyone's worst fears—was an overwhelming success. Patti had expected to be intimidated by the large audience and the presence of the camera crew from KPUX. But with the exception of the first few minutes, her confidence never wavered.

The music swelled around her, full and sweet, as they launched into Mendelssohn's *Elijah.* Tim's voice floated up from the tenor section. Then it was Patti's turn. She opened up, pouring her heart and soul into each note.

She could tell, from Mr. Reese's beaming expression, that she was projecting far enough. Once she glanced over and caught Tim looking at her. The pride that shone from his eyes filled her with a warm glow. Being on TV wasn't the important thing, she realized—it was knowing she had done her best that really counted.

As pleased as she was with her own performance, however, Patti was stunned by the surge of enthusiastic applause that greeted the finish of the piece. Mr. Reese motioned for the soloists to step down and take their bows. Patti was only dimly aware of Tim grabbing her hand.

"You're the real star," he murmured as they

moved to center stage and the camera dollied forward to focus on their faces.

At that exact moment, right in front of everyone, with the camera's eye pointed straight at them, Tim kissed her lightly on the lips. Patti blushed, and a half dozen hoots and wolf whistles could be heard above the clapping.

He mouthed the words, "I love you."

Patti's eyes filled, but Tim's face remained clear and bright for a long, searching moment before melting into the blur around her.

Frank Curtis battled his way through the admiring crush, Tim's petite mother in tow, to envelop his daughter in a smothering hug.

"Beverly Sills, move over!" he crowed, beaming with fatherly pride.

As Mr. Curtis turned to shake Tim's hand in congratulations, Ann McBride, looking very elegant in a burgundy suit and ruffled pink blouse, stood on tiptoe to plant a quick peck on Patti's cheek.

"Congratulations, Patti, you were wonderful!"

And then, as Mrs. McBride turned to her son to embrace him for his fine performance, Tim shot his mother a questioning look, to which she responded saucily, "Oh, don't look so shocked. I knew she was a girl after my own heart the night we met. Plenty of spunk, the way she stood up to you like that." She winked at Patti. "We women have to stick together, right?"

Mr. Curtis pretended to be crushed. "And all this time I thought it was my manly influence that turned you around."

"You're absolutely incorrigible, Frank Curtis!" She turned to address Patti. "Do you know what your father did? In case you're wondering how the two of us ever managed to get together without killing each other—"

"I lured her over to our house under false pretenses," he supplied, chuckling.

Ann bridled but couldn't resist a wicked smile of her own. "Of all the dirty tricks—"

"Listen to the expert!" he parried.

"This one really takes the cake. Calling me up to tell me my son is over at your house and isn't budging until I come over and talk to you. Honestly!"

"Worked, didn't it?"

"I certainly wasn't about to let him miss the concert!"

"You didn't really think I'd go on strike, did you, Mom?" asked Tim.

She grinned sheepishly. "I guess I wasn't thinking. I panicked."

"I know the feeling," Patti mumbled.

"Anyway," Mr. Curtis put in, "once she got her feathers unruffled, we had a nice long talk. Tim, your mother's quite a talker."

Ann shot him a suspicious look. "I'm not sure that's a compliment, coming from you. Just keep in mind who's driving you home, Frank Curtis."

"I will," he promised, "if you remember who your insurance agent is."

Ann shrugged, smiling at Tim and Patti. "What can I say? He made me an offer I couldn't refuse."

"I was at her mercy," he protested. "All that trouble to get her over there, and I find out my car won't start. I had to bribe Ann somehow into giving me a ride, or I would've missed the concert."

"Bribe nothing," she retorted. "I simply couldn't resist the pleasure of picking up a knight who'd fallen off his horse."

Frank threw up his hands with a roar. "OK, OK, I surrender. Looks like you women have me surrounded, so I might as well give in graciously. How about letting this dusty knight buy you a drink on the way home, Ann? Consider it my way of waving the white flag."

"Well—" She hesitated.

"Strictly business, of course," he added, his eyes twinkling. "I'll even let you open your own doors."

As Patti and Tim stared at each other in delighted astonishment, Ann pronounced, "You've got yourself a date. But how about all of us going somewhere together? I hear they make great pepperoni pies down at the Pizza Palace."

"We'd like to," Tim said, "but Mr. Reese is having a party over at his house. Then a bunch of us are going over to the Gulch to hear that new guitarist—"

"Enough," Mr. Curtis cut in, "I get the picture! We old folks will manage without you."

"Is that OK with you, Dad?" Patti asked.

"On one condition—"

"Uh-oh," she added, then laughed. "I think I know what's coming!"

"I want Tim to *drive carefully!*"

Tim slipped an arm about Patti's shoulders, and as she looked up into his laughing blue eyes, the old electricity zapped her in the pit of her stomach. Except it was all OK now. No more hiding, more sneaking around. Of course, she never would have gone so far as

to hope her father and Ann might be friends—
but then, who would have believed a dented
bumper could bring Tim and her together in
the first place?

His eyes never leaving her face, Tim smiled
and answered, "With pleasure."

We hope you enjoyed reading this book. Some of the titles currently available in the Sweet Dreams series are listed on the next page. They are all available at your local bookshop or newsagent, though should you find any difficulty in obtaining the books you would like, you can order direct from the publisher, at the address below. Also, if you would like to know more about the series, or would simply like to tell us what you think of the series, write to:

Kim Prior,
Sweet Dreams,
Transworld Publishers Limited,
Century House,
61—63 Uxbridge Road,
London W5 5SA.

or
Kiri Martin
c/o Corgi & Bantam Books New Zealand,
9 Waipareira Avenue,
Henderson,
Auckland,
New Zealand.

To order books, please list the title(s) you would like, and send together with your name and address, and a cheque or postal order made payable to TRANSWORLD PUBLISHERS LIMITED. Please allow cost of book(s) plus 20p for the first book and 10p for each additional book for postage and packing.